Marriage without Marriage

Marriage without Marriage

S.K. SOOD

LiFi Publications Pvt. Ltd.
New Delhi

Published by:
LiFi Publications Pvt. Ltd.
211, 2nd Floor, Gagandeep
12, Rajendra Place, New Delhi–110 008, India
Phone : (011) 2574 1000
E-mail : info@lifipublications.com
Web : www.lifipublications.com

ISBN 13: 978-93-82536-15-4 ISBN 10: 93-82536-15-9

First published in 2015

Cataloging in Publication Data—DK
[Courtesy: D.K. Agencies (P) Ltd. <docinfo@dkagencies.com>]

Sood, S. K. (Sumod Kumar), 1947–
Marriage without marriage / S.K. Sood.
p. cm.
Novel.
ISBN 9789382536154

1. School employees--Fiction. 2. Marriage--Fiction. 3. Indic fiction (English). I. Title.

DDC 823.92 23

Printed in India by D.K. Fine Art Press (P) Ltd., Delhi–52.

Dedicated to
my sweet grand children
Prachi Sood and Archit Sood
who always cooperated in the project
of novel writing
and also guided me off and on
as to what was really good
from their point of view

Contents

Acknowledgement

Different writers may present the names of different individuals in this auspicious column and express their gratitude to those who have gone a long way to make a particular work happen and see the light of the day. The most often quoted names are parents, wives, beloveds, gods and goddesses, friends and teachers etc. They are right and I admit and admire their sense of gratitude and regards for those who inspired them to achieve distinction in the world of letters. I am beholden to all of the above mentioned people. All of them have been, to a lesser or greater degree, my inspirers and are responsible for inspiring me in all my works.

But the chief source of my inspiration, the one of which I must make mention is:

Aye Gardishe Ayam Tera Sukria

Hamne Her Pahlu Se Dunia Dekh Lee!

Translated into English I would put it in the words of William Shakespeare as:

"Sweet are the uses of Adversity."

To my mind, perhaps, the luckiest people in the world are those who are born in poverty, live in poverty and die in poverty. Out of their poverty they leave behind writers like Munshi Prem Chand. "Foot prints on the sands of time which may act in times to come as source of unending inspiration and prosperity for a less fortunate human being."

Another laudable contributor is the LiFi Publications who have always have faith in the budding writers, who provided them the platform to climb new horizons in the literary world.

I

Exploiting the Helplessness

"Catch her legs.
Gag her mouth.
Tear her blouse.
Use your force.
Bite her cheeks.
We are four of us.
Hale and hearty.
Besides we are drunk,
Can't we handle this frail girl?
We must not miss this golden opportunity.
Fix her hard.
Let us all maul her, one by one.
Together.
No one will come here.
It is 5 a.m., chilly-drizzling December morning,"
sang the first rapist.

"Ouch!" cried the don of the gang, Natha.

"I am done. She has bitten me hard! I cannot stand on my legs. I am all bleeding."

He started yelling like the one who had been rolled down a cliff into a gorge, and disappeared into the dark.

I pushed a hard punch into the stomach of the second hound whose face resembled a ruffian having the darkest design.

I had learnt Judo in my high school days and had won special proficiency in it.

I had won the black belt also.

Blood gushed forth his mouth as a boy given to an overdose of smack, who vomits rather violently.

Without uttering a single word, he ran as fast as his addicted legs could carry him.

The remaining two, thought they were near achieving their nefarious deed.

The stouter of the two, who had liquor drenched moustache, and an ugly pimpled face, took out a dagger from his side hurling it into my face, he thundered, "Durga my darling! I had a crush on you ever since you were eight and I thirty."

He brought the knife right under my neck sliding it between my breasts and said, "If you do not submit of your own accord, we will pierce your heart, take out your entrails, and satisfy our lust with your dead body. But mind you, we will have our fill of sex today in the wee hours of this morning."

I somersaulted at a lightning speed. And without any intention I ended up hitting the forehead of the third goon with my high heels, wounding his eye beyond repair.

He did not expect such arduous display of action from an Indian girl, at least.

The fourth scoundrel, by now had known that he was no match to my agility, muscle power and expertise in Judo.

Falling on my feet, he cringed, "Durga we hail from the same colony. I have always looked upon you as a sister. Please spare my life!"

Putting on his underwear he struggled to pick the last piece of clothing, and disappeared into the dark.

An animal as he was, was chased by stray dogs, which pounced on him, punishing him suitably.

Left alone, I thanked the goddess. Lifting my broken cycle, I headed for the Primary School, Gangual where I had been appointed as a temporary teacher a week ago.

My daily journey started with boarding a train at 4 a.m., and after that, I would start pedalling to my place of posting, 5 km away.

Rain, hail or storm, I had to report for duty before 7 a.m. and late, even by 10 minutes, meant dismissal from service. All my seniors were looking for opportunities to point fingers at me and leave me in a thick soup. A temporary teacher, as I was, it was difficult to prove myself amidst the old, established lot.

Unemployment is a curse. Because of this, some people even don't mind taking their own lives. We read more news about suicidal deaths because of unemployment than success stories of people gainfully employed.

Though initially temporary, my job in this government school was liable to be made permanent if everything about me was found to be satisfactory from all perspectives.

From all perspectives!

It had a large number of connotations when a very pretty and young teacher like me was the topic of discussion.

The school was under the charge of the elected headman of the village. He was supposed to supervise the performance of all teachers and maintain a record of their activities, summing them up into a yearly performance report before the expiry of the year. This then became the decisive factor for the confirmation of a teacher's job.

The headman was to be satisfied, academically. This included the quality of teaching, the amount of interest the teacher could generate in children and the teacher's awareness level.

The irony of the situation was that whereas he was to see the educational efficiency of the newly appointed teacher, he himself was a consistent third division all the time; sometimes had made two attempts to pass a single class.

Then there were the DEO, the CEO and a host of other officers who additionally looked into the confirmation aspect.

A few of them, if not all, were like the members of the gang I had encountered in the paddy fields.

I just inspected myself to see if everything about me was presentable and just then I spotted drops of blood on my shirt, the result of the violent scuffle with the ruffians.

'What do I do now?' I wondered.

Going to the school would mean a spiteful encounter with the headmaster. Though they called him Ram, it was only namesake. The man was a sure incarnation of Ravana.

He would make hundred stories and give currency to those in the entire area and the news of my gang rape, which I had so bravely evaded, would be the hot cake. Thoughts kept flashing through: how would I ever wash off the sins that were never mine! It would become difficult for me to wash the blame so attached to my character.

I looked at my old broken watch. Everything in it was as if belonged to some hoary past. All was wrong with this – the strap, the dials, the wings, etc. Only thing it kept correct was time. By now, it had stopped drizzling. I knew a rivulet that ran on my way to the school.

Carefully parking my cycle on one side, I looked around to check if there was anyone. Sure of no human soul around, I took off my shirt and bent over the water. My own reflection smiled at me.

My face was finely chiselled like an alabaster statue. I was thankful to God for making me beautiful.

I had about 50 minutes more with me. I washed my shirt off and hung it to drip dry, carefully hiding myself beneath the foliage. I did not want to be seen by any one. Nothing connected with me was visible, except my broken bicycle.

My shirt, I had spread on the branches so as to get maximum air, it fluttered as if wanting to break free.

My cycle, I called it 'darling' was indispensable and I felt as useless without it as it would feel without me. The more I looked at it, the more I was reminded of the circumstances of how it had come in my possession. It was a long time back.

I fell into a reverie.

My father in a delusional drunken state was threatening to kill every member of the family, about ten years back, after a family brawl.

I was in class eight then; an impressionable mind, unaware of the worldly ways.

There were not many members to be killed in the family. Tormented by a drunken spouse all the years had erased any visible signs of life from my mother's body and soul. Besides, my only brother was polio affected since he was three. While my grandfather had passed away when my father was barely four days old, my grandmother drowned herself in a canal soon after.

The only person who, he could kill was me. And it would not have been a difficult task since he had no love for me. He had no love for his wife; he treated every mortal soul around him with the same hatred.

He had been a total failure in his life. He was neither sent to a school nor did he show any inclination to study. He had spent his whole life in the same one room accommodation and probably planned to breathe his last there. He shifted a score of professions; however addiction to alcohol failed him in all his endeavours. Similar was the fate of his attempts to quit alcohol. He became a victim of his addiction and this helplessness made him sympathise only with himself. Finally, he gave in completely, not making any efforts to get rid of alcoholism. A question that never left my mind was why he was not asked to vacate the house in spite of his nasty habit of getting drunk. The question was all the more important since after drinking he would make a lot of fuss and create nuisance. He would almost become a hazard. Still he was granted the liberty to spend his life in the same house.

The house was shunned by all and we never had any visitors. People were too afraid even to pass across our house especially after midnight, as it was rumoured that goblins danced on the peepal tree, in the street opposite our house.

As for us, we lived amicably with the ghost, though no one ever saw it. None troubled the other.

The worst affected member of the family was I, Durga. A pretty girl must never be born to a poor family! It is the greatest curse; total damnation and Lord take mercy on the girl!

I was hardly 10, when I noticed the way men looked at me – men aged 19 to 90. Back then, I could not interpret their gaze, but it strangely scared me.

In class 5, I met an excellent teacher, Miss Ragini. She was 40 and still a spinster. It was difficult for her to find a husband who would accept her without dowry. For a teacher in a private school it was a torture, mental and financial, of the worst kind. She could not wear well, eat well or go out to spend leisure time with her friends and relatives. Finances severely held her family back all the time.

Miss Ragini tried her luck with bachelors, divorcees and men double her age. Invariably, rejection was the case. It was made out that she neither was rich nor beautiful and therefore must remain a spinster and die so. Besides, her mother was a public dancer, who was looked down upon. But all this never dampened her spirits. She always talked to me with love and consideration and taught me many valuable things. She often quoted Swami Vivekananda:

'Strength is life, weakness is death.'

She very often narrated the immortal story of Hemingway's novel 'The Old Man and the Sea' to the class. She was a wonderful story teller, and would put life and soul into the imaginary story of Santiago. She taught us never to lose courage whatever the circumstances may be.

She told us how the old man struggled for more than thirty years, to catch a Merlin and how he ultimately succeeded in it. Perseverance was the key. What mattered was how much courage we put into the fight and how strong our determination to win was.

She would often quote Napoleon the great, 'Life is the courage we bring to bear upon it.'

Her watchwords were the lines from Robert Browning,

'As the bird wings and sings,
Let us cry, all good things are ours,
nor soul helps flesh more,
now, than flesh helps soul?'

What a perfect teacher Miss Ragini was. She ensured that all her students excelled. She carved out of them soldiers of strength, and made them perfect epitomes of feminity.

I was Miss Ragini's favourite disciple. I loved and worshipped her, though she was neither beautiful nor rich.

What has beauty or riches got to do with being a good person?

The proverb, 'Handsome is what handsome does,' is absolutely true.

Besides, she instilled in me the fact that virtue was a woman's most precious possession. One must never succumb to sexual attraction with anybody. A woman must remember herself as a human being, the highest and the noblest creation of God and not a beast, ridden with lust and animality.

With the passage of time, I developed into a paragon of beauty, inch by inch and contour by contour. My father did not pay even a cent for my education. He couldn't have as he never acknowledged his role as the man of the house. Even if he could acknowledge, how would he give any money? He was a waster who spent any petty amount he earned in gambling, drinking and even womanising.

The total expenditure of my education was borne by Non-Governmental Organisations. The world is inhabited by all sorts of people – good and wicked. The good never falter in helping others. While wicked never falter to take advantage of the good ones and condemn them.

With all the assistance I got, I expressed my gratitude through my hard work. I was as studious as I was beautiful. Different philanthropist organisations always came forward to help me monetarily with books, even with clothes and other expenses connected with education. For many years, I did not feel the shortage of any kind of funds for my education, whether it was an amount of Rs. 5000 or more; The Rotary Club, The Lions Club, The Bharat Vikas Parishad, all these organisations vied with one another to help me reach my goal. They did not want anything in return except my good performance which in the ultimate analysis again helped me.

I remained a distinction holder throughout. All my teachers went out of the way to help me in every possible way. I was mostly an outstanding student in all the schools and colleges where I studied. My hostel room was well decorated with a large number of shields, trophies and certificates which I earned at various levels. I became a science graduate and my B.Ed was the cherry on the cake.

Soon after, I did my Masters in English, privately with the help of Prof. Sood at Siali Road. The professor also, acknowledging my skills and calibre did not charge any money and I worked hard to keep his honour high, securing the III position in the final examination. I was now eligible for the post of a teacher/lecturer.

Sports interested me equally as studies and I excelled there as well, particularly in Judo.

Once, I went out of town for an inter college Judo match. I had to share the bed with Kamini. At midnight, in deep sleep, I felt someone touching my breasts.

Stirred out of sleep, I shouted, "What are you doing Kamini? I don't like all this. I will complain against you to the Principal and tell the whole college about this or else you must behave."

She withdrew and acted as if I had miscalculated and she did not have such intentions. I too, for a second, thought that I would have been mistaken. What had a woman to do with a woman, both being of the same sex?

Sexual interaction between the two made no sense to me as opposed to the same between opposite sexes. Though I had heard about LGBT studies and their fight for equal rights.

Moreover, as advised by my teacher Miss Ragini, I did not pay any attention to this topic; instead my focus was on my studies. Probably that was what helped me excel.

Beyond that, I dedicated the left over time to the ferocious game of Judo.

In matters of sex, my knowledge was nearly nil. I was a total novice, but I did understand the sexual union of a male and a female. I did know about lesbianism, homosexuality and other aberration of sex, but I never even let the thought to creep into my mind since I had bigger goals to achieve in life.

The G.T. Road for me led straight to my training centre. Thinking that I might have hurt her sentiments, I regretted, 'Kamini, I am sorry. I just spoke hard to you.' I covered myself and her with the same blanket and was in deep slumber in minutes. The trend there was to give a single quilt or blanket, large enough to accommodate two persons.

Suddenly, I was startled into awakening when she placed her lips on mine and tried to fondle my breasts just one hour after the previous encounter. I felt she had become warm and was perspiring. I at once hurried out of the bed. Checked time. It was 4 a.m. Taking a deep breath I focused my mind on the match.

Since the match was scheduled at 8 a.m., I massaged my body, did some exercises, ignoring Kamini's presence in the room throughout. Finally I mediated and was ready for the

Judo finals. I won the match though like all finals it was a tough fight.

I never said anything to Kamini for I did not know what her compulsion was. Everybody is a product of his/her circumstances. She thanked me by hugging so tightly that my ribs broke.

I came back to the present with this.

A quick whiff of wind blew away my shirt from the branches onto the grass. I tiptoed to catch the shirt, cautious enough not to be seen by anyone. Putting it on, I started for the school.

I cycled my way to school and reached just in time, the headmaster showed up. We exchanged glances and I could see the mischief in his eyes.

"What is the latest about the old man?" he taunted intending to ask about my father.

"I learnt he had a row with some drunkards in the pub and was detained in the police station," detailed the headmaster insultingly. Without caring to answer, I moved to the other room to meet my students.

The schools in far flung areas in India are uncared for; those at the primary level are the worst hit. Our school was no exception. With no proper seating, the students either accommodated themselves on the tattered mats or on the floor itself. One room had no windows, and the other, no roof.

I learnt that during the rainy seasons, poisonous reptiles and sometimes even venomous snakes paid visit to the school as it was set up amidst the fields.

I entered the dark and dingy room that accommodated 73 students, most of them unwilling to study, and gathered because the government wanted to show an increased literacy rate through crowded classrooms.

I started with the basic alphabet of English language and had barely reached 'n' when the headmaster barged into the classroom rather insultingly and questioned rudely, "Is it how you write the alphabet? None of your letters is properly written. If you yourself cannot write the alphabet correctly, how would you teach the language to the students? Come to my office after the class."

The loafer way with which he left for his office made matters clear to me.

God has blessed women folk with instinctive qualities which he has probably denied all others in his creation. It is the intuitive power given to the fairer sex to know and understand unmistakably, the intentions of their male counterpart, if those are not in the gentleman's way.

Luckily, there was another female teacher Balwant Kaur in the same school. There was some difference between us, the only two female teachers. She was in her forties while I was in my twenties. Secondly, she was a permanent teacher with vast experience. Her services could not be terminated easily. There was a rather cumbersome procedure to terminate the services of a permanent teacher. I was not only temporary but also a new recruit. My services could be terminated by the headmaster without citing any reason.

I went to her classroom, adjoining mine; a far better room. The permanent appointment, entitled her a better treatment in everything. Even in as trivial matters as allocation of chalks. I was to write with poor quality chalks whereas Balwant Kaur would write with deluxe quality chalks.

The headmaster's mean thoughts sent a shiver down my spine. I sought her help. I said to her, "Sister, I need you to guide me! Could you tell me how to deal with the headmaster? Even though I had won prizes and awards, not only at the district level but state level as well for my expertise in hand writing, the headmaster thought it befitting to condemn me before the students and has asked to see me after the class."

I continued further, "Instinctively, I know what his intentions are! Though, I can deal with ten ruffians like him to defend my honour, but here the case is slightly different. My work and character await his certification for a permanent job. I have already suffered enough hardships at his hand...what else now!"

I could hear the desperation in my own voice.

Balwant Kaur was a Punjabi woman and like all other Punjabis she was ready to help.

To my surprise she suggested that I should hold the headmaster, pull him down from his chair and thrash him with the sandals. She further announced, "And in this great enterprise, I would be happy to join you. An unholy man like him needs to be taken to task." Though the thought deeply delighted me, I thought it unwise to go all out for it right away.

I was militarily trained in the martial arts. True! But I was a true Gandhian above all. I wanted to explore all possibilities.

Just then the bell rang. As I was preparing to go to meet the headmaster, the school peon Mota Ram came running to me and said, "There is a message for you from the headmaster sir." He said, "You needn't meet him, besides your handwriting is also pretty fine." Saying so the peon went away, leaving me completely shocked.

It was only after a few months that I came to know the reason for the sudden change in the behaviour of the headmaster. He had seen me talking to Balwant Kaur and was petrified at the thought of being roughed up by two fiery women. It also became clear that he had tasted defeat earlier, while trying to misbehave with Balwant Kaur when she was a temporary teacher.

Even as a temporary teacher, Balwant Kaur had the nerve not only to push him into the drain but also shower sandals and parade him around, which he had not forgotten till date. Probably his head ached at the very thought of the incident.

Sitting alone in the broken staff room chair I was lost in deep thought.

'What if those four scoundrels who tried to rape me in the paddy fields were to return? Men who are foiled in their sexual desires become as ferocious as mad dogs. It goes hard with sexually rebuffed and drunkards to accept defeat.'

'What if they brought more ruffians for support?'

'What could I do?' I felt myself alone today!

Alone, Alone,

All Alone,

Alone in the wide world!

If I talked to my father about the incident, he would talk casually about it and drink two large pegs to sleep over the issue. Talking to my polio affected brother would be of no help. He could barely stand on his legs, expecting him to be braving and fighting those ruffians out with knives, would be like mocking him.

I was grown up enough, and most of the girls of my age had around a dozen affairs, true or false. However, I never felt any amorous feelings for any one so far. I was yet to come across the hero of my dreams.

Through Judo, I had close encounters only with girls. I had come to believe that both friendship and enmity between two women was stronger than that between two men, by all standards.

I had a very close pal in one of my Judo mates. Whenever we went as a team to fight, I chose her, the Haryanvi girl Sneha as the partner. We generally won. I told her of my predicament.

She was furious, "Durga! Don't waste words. Come straight to the point. You know I can give my life for you. What do you want me to do for you?"

I told Sneha of the whole incident in the fields. She was only too agitated, "Don't worry! I shall come with you. We together can face the world."

She always made light of the situation by uttering a funny word or two. "If a scuffle takes place, I may have to fall up or down over any one of them. Is any one of them handsome? I have heard some of the villains too have the softest hearts and most handsome faces. I shall first choose the villain I would like and then give him the taste of my fists..."

"Ha! Ha! Ha!" we laughed.

In fact, we had another support, on which we could depend in face of any danger, our young Judo instructor, Harkamal Singh! He also carried a licensed revolver with him. Brave and daring, he had only two fascinations in the world, helping the ones in danger and thrashing the wicked.

But we thought of not bothering him for an issue like dealing with the drunkards unless they surfaced with barbaric intentions. We thought ourselves to be enough for them.

We had a plan. While I cycled ahead Sneha followed me closely. Patiently, we waited for those ruffians at the place of the incident, but none of them showed up. May be they were just dressing their wounds or advising others not to meddle with women. Days passed, then weeks and months, they never came that side.

True! Indian women had descended from the lineage of Queen of Jhansi, and were certainly dangerous if meddled with.

Accompanying me on several occasions, Sneha finally decided and said, "May be those bastards have learnt the lessons of their lives from you alone and have not dared to show up again."

Then on, I went on myself. Over time, I realised that all teachers were not as wicked as the headmaster. Many teachers I came across were not only genuine but also made me take pride in my profession.

Soon everyone in the district came to know that a very pretty, young teacher had joined the school at Gangual. More and more villagers became keen and got their children for admission to the school. Those who were bachelors or had no children of their own came with others' children pretending they were doing so for the cause of education.

In fact, they just wanted to interact with me for a while and enjoy the bliss of a conversation with a dedicated teacher like me.

'A thing of beauty is a joy forever,' I laughed.

In the same village, a member of the block committee took fancy for me. He used to stand in the way, I generally followed. He talked to his protégée about my charm and wanted to make an effort.

On a Saturday, in connivance with headmaster Ram, they cornered me in the school, near its closing time. They bribed the peon and sent him to enjoy the circus along with his family. The peon was delighted to leave.

I was asked to hold on for 15 minutes as the member wanted to have some important discussion on the new educational guidelines and my job. I had no choice but to wait and listen to them.

The member started, "Durga it is about a year now that you have been serving this school. Your probationary period is just ending day after. What is needed is a certificate of your good character and moral conduct from the headmaster to be counter signed by me. We have come here together to do the honours. Don't lament later that you were not warned!"

I was getting anxious and beginning to suspect their intentions. Bending forward, he went on,"I am a very frank and honest man. I practice no underhand methods. I hate being unkind to women. They are the weaker sex. We must help and respect them." I could sense the heaviness of his breath under the increasing politeness.

"I hate to use force or pressure. It is a simple give and take. You please us and we please you. Think of what you have to lose? No one will know it. No trace of it remains on the body of a woman. Your gain is enormous. Lifelong salary and food for you and your polio hit brother. Even your future generations will stand to gain."

I could feel blood rushing in my veins...the heat emanating from my checks was surely giving them a pink tinge. I could feel that my eyes were beginning to swell.

Shamelessly he added, "A girl does not find a husband these days if she does not have a permanent job. By just giving in once you will have a life full of comforts. Then marriage may be, within a month. Don't miss the golden opportunity. Otherwise, we know how to use force also."

I had to hold back my emotions. I had thought deep enough. Judo is a game that not only gives agility of the body but also superb quick-wittedness. I said, as if meditatively, "Sir, today the weather is very hot and unromantic. Moreover my probation period ends day after. I agree to your great words of wisdom. I hope you would be kind in a similar manner towards your daughter, had she been awaiting a similar certificate. Yes, by going into a sexual union a woman does not lose anything! Great! I am in total agreement." Brimming with confidence, I added, "I agree to your wish, of my own sweet will. In order to honour your great service of providing me and my helpless family with food and shelter for the rest of our lives. I shall only be too glad to do whatever you want. But one man one woman. One woman one man. That is ideal. You are two of you. You will however have to agree to two of my conditions."

They seemed to be prepared to agreeing to two hundred of my conditions because, 'Beauty provokes thieves more than gold'.

They were quick, "What are your conditions? What are those? What?"

I relaxed back and laid out my conditions, "We will do it day after, when the two of you have signed the satisfactory report document in triplicate; one to be posted to the DEO, second for the Education Secretary and the third for me duly endorsed and given diary number. You will present that to me as a gift in lieu of my anticipated cohabitation with you. Then my friend Sneha and I will present us to you as a gift in return of your act of kindness. The rest, we will celebrate after a good dinner.

"Remember it should be a delicious dinner. The two of us are virgins and it must be celebrated properly. I choose you, headmaster sir for the great moment. You have three children, two grown up daughters and are quite experienced. You experienced men prove better with women, I think." Turning to the member, I said "You, sir should accept my friend. After the certificate job being satisfactorily done, we shall be at your pleasure in City Hotel room at 6 p.m. But remember, we shall not let any third man touch any part of our body. Do you agree?"

Thrilled at the offer, the duo spoke together, "Yes, we swear by our honour to fulfill your conditions, in letter and spirit."

Leaving the room, the headmaster turned back with his anecdote, "Gold does not get cheaper anyway just if people touch it."

They left weaving golden dreams about the anticipated sexual pleasures. I met Sneha and requested her to accommodate that guy for just an hour or so. It would just be a cake walk the day after in the hotel room.

'A woman should boldly face any situation if it arrives and try to teach the assaulter a lesson for a lifetime so that he thinks twice before planning to shame a woman.' She thought.

Two of us reached the majestic City Hotel in time. There, we learnt that the duo had been hanging around the rooms since three o'clock, many hours in advance for understandable reasons.

We walked across the long corridor to the lobby outside the rooms. Not even best pals would greet each other, the way we were greeted.

Maintaining my charming smile, I asked the headmaster, "Have you placed the order for the dinner? And, have you brought the certificate with proper diary number?"

The headmaster showed me the letter, and I was fully satisfied. It was only to be signed by the headmaster and the member and I wanted it to be signed in my presence so as to avoid any kind of cheating.

The member, Sukh Lal said, "You two are really very pretty girls. You relax here for a while, have a look at the certificate and see if anything more is to be added while we will come back after a couple of drinks."

During this time, we planned what was to be done. We decided to sort them out most tactfully.

They returned to the dinner table heavily drunk, barely able to talk. Dinner was served and it was taken rather hurriedly by the men as they wanted to get set to the most important work, right away. We relished it taking our own time.

With my best smile on, I looked at the headmaster, "Now that the dinner is over, please sign the certificates so that we will get on with the most important part of the evening."

The headmaster twisted his mouth a bit and replied, "We are happy to tell you that it is with pleasure that we are putting the signatures on the documents. It entitles you for a regular job." Sneha's brother, himself a state boxer, took away the signed documents and disappeared in a jiffy leaving behind a small container and a brush. The duo was aghast and their jaws dropped as I announced, "You are a set of shameless bastards. My friend and I are University champions in Judo.

"We will first take out your teeth and then paint your faces black. Donkeys are on their way to give you a good ride through the streets of the town. We are also sending for your wives and daughters to come here and witness the great scene."

All drunken loafers can be taught the lesson of their lives. They are not brave. They are worst cowards. In fact anybody on the wrong foot cannot face the brave, just, right and the virtuous.

✦ ✦ ✦

II

Tables Turned

When the lusty bastards sensed that the tables had turned, they thought it fit to wriggle out of the situation and save their skin. The headmaster fell at my feet, "Durga, please forgive us. I admit that we are a pack of ruffians. If you create a scene, we will not be able to show our faces in the society nor will we be able to face our families." The member begged too, "I am an elected member of the town. What will the people of my constituency think? Please, for God's sake, forgive us."

Their words began to repeat and echo in the room, "We will be ruined for all times to come. It will be difficult for me to find husbands for my three daughters.

"I shall never ever think of such an act again, leave alone doing it." I was reminded of my teacher Ragini who could not find a husband and how she suffered alone in this world. Finally, she had to become a nun.

Slapping both of them hard to give them a taste of the woman power, I took hold of the box of paint, and held out the brush with the black paint, just then both of them fell at my feet and cringed in most pathetic manner. Both of them said as if in unison, "You are like our daughter! We have committed an outrageous sin by behaving in the most wretched and mean manner. We are not humans. We are dogs. We are poisonous serpents. But please, forgive us once and we will never come your way."

The mention of their families and daughters had become their saviours. We took pity on them and let them go after a little sandal parade. We were very happy and thanked our Judo teacher, Harkamal who had given us strength enough to deal with the wicked specimens of humanity.

I thanked Sneha with all my heart, "This dose should be enough for them. Both of them are responsible citizens. One is the headmaster and the other is an elected representative of the people. They will be reformed in their work, conduct and character in future. I am glad to have a friend like you!" Hugging her I said, "I am very happy. We have got our work done and at the same time reformed two fallen debauched human beings."

I started looking at the certificates.

The duo's repentance was only to save their skin at that time. The headmaster along with the member had crossed the bridge. Conspiring against me, the headmaster said to the member, "Sir, this bitch Durga has insulted us like anything. She has slapped us most barbarously. I swear never to forget this insult and never to forgive her. I'll always be on the look out for an opportunity, to fuck her or mortally harm her drunkard father, wretched mother and if not anybody else, her crippled brother." He roared furiously, "My soul will rest in peace only when I satisfy my lust with her."

The member too, was agitated enough, "I agree with you, completely. We will together carve the destruction of her life and career as the only and exclusive aim of our life at whatever cost."

The next day, when I was reading an advertisement in the newspaper regarding the position of a teacher at a very big school near Solan, I saw a few boys running up to the school. They told me that some wicked people had attacked my invalid brother Jaggi.

Instinctively, I knew it was a reaction to yesterday's hotel incident. I at once ran to my brother's rescue. Thank God, he was only bruised a little. By the intervention of some courageous and compassionate people at the place of brawl, he was saved. I took him home. I was boiling inside and thought if I should lodge an F.I.R. against the duo. But I was not sure of whom the assailants were. It was, I thought, proper to wait and watch and be more cautious and careful in future. I advised my brother, not to go far away from the house alone under any circumstances. But I had decided not to risk the life of any member of my family.

I must go next Sunday for the interview and join the job if I get selected, at the earliest. Although I was not at all hopeful of getting it since I did not have any approach or godfather in the selection committee. In India, these extraneous influences are more necessary than the qualifications itself. Nonetheless, I decided to go and attend the interview.

There were around 12 to 13 candidates from probably the whole of northern India for the interview. There were specific reasons, I understood, for the interviewees to come in that large number. In the first instance, the school, Mother India was one of the best schools in the area in academics, co-curricular activities, cultural and sports fields. It was, at preference above all with the parents far and wide. The students were taken on merit. Understandably, they showed good results.

The management of the school was at one time in the hands of Smt. Vidyawati, the wife of the Chairman of the Group of Paper Mills, Mr. Romesh Chadda. But that was twenty years ago.

With the passage of time, I learnt, brought a lot of changes in the school. Today, it had developed into a huge and spacious structure from what used to be a shadow of its present self. It rose to three storey with at least 73 rooms, an auditorium, playgrounds, hostel, swimming pools, gym, and above all a meditation centre for everybody, a student, a teacher or even an outsider who took interest.

The strength of the students had risen from paltry fifty to three thousand. The turn of events had also raised its level from an earlier pre primary to now, a full fledged Higher Secondary school, one of the best of its kind in the district.

Mr. Romesh Chadda did not have ample time left from his business for the school. But, his wife, Smt. Vidyawati proved to be a great manager and a greater administrator.

Mr. Chadda gave donations to the school generously; partly because he was a philanthropic person and partly because it saved him money under some sections of the income tax. Unfortunately, a silent heart attack took his life rather unexpectedly.

Smt. Vidyawati administration was the golden period in the life history of the school. She was completely devoted and deeply involved with all the activities of the school herself.

However, she was consumed from inside after the death of her husband. She became weaker day by day and finally one night left to be with her husband in the other world.

"Candidate number 2 please come inside the office," the secretary's voice interrupted my thoughts. I saw a pompous lady walk into the office. None could tell her age from her looks.

I was scheduled at number 11. It must be a four hour wait at least, given that every candidate was being interviewed for some 25 minutes.

The wait however helped me understand my prospective work place better. I learnt that the school was at present, passing through its worst phase. Mr. Chadda's son Vishal, himself an MBA from New York, had no time for the school, considering the vast business empire left to him. Despite his interest in the school, he very rarely, came over. At 24 he was still a bachelor. It was by sheer chance; that he was today chairing the selection committee. In fact, it was his opinion today that was to matter. And, they said that he was a man who cared for merit alone.

My confidence came alive and I thought, 'If the selection is made on merit, I may stand a chance. I can speak good English and my communication skills were extremely mature. I have good general awareness. Besides, I have been a topper in almost all my exams. My co-curricular interests were also appreciable. Along with a black belt in Judo, I was a classical dancer and singer too. But the best thing about me, I was aware, was that I was a Lydian beauty.'

I knew I was beautiful and that made me more confident. Needless to say that chastity lent dignity to the grace.

My number was finally called out and I entered the interview room.

The bard of Avon has rightly said: 'Who ever loved that loved not at first sight?'

The moment Vishal looked at me he was as clearly stung by my charm. As for me, he seemed my quest for love and fulfillment, though till then I had not known what love or fulfillment really meant. Taking hold of himself, he asked, "What is your name ma'am?" It was the first question asked by him, but he looked straight into my eyes.

I was also swept off my feet by his good looks and grace.

I forgot what my name was. Something had happened to me. It was after a second that I said, "My name is Durga." Inadvertently, I too looked into his eyes. That made him forget who he was and where he was.

After that it was interview in the earnest. I surprised the committee with my intelligence, quick-wittedness and cordial responses.

"I think you can sing as well," asked Vishal, looking through my CV.

"Yes I can," I replied.

"What can you sing?" another member of the selection committee asked.

"Anything from a religious prayer to ghazals and bollywood songs."

"Does your martial art protect you at times? I mean if there are three or four persons misbehaving with you, can you guard your honour," asked a third member. I explained my beliefs on women empowerment and how girls should be equipped with this art to protect themselves from the ruffians that abound the society, cornering women on streets, near schools and colleges to molest young girls in the rudest possible way. Those bastards should be shown what a strong well educated and Judo trained girl can do. All this came spontaneously and later I repented the use of the word bastard in a formal interview.

"Very good," the Chairman said, "In our school, the girls outnumber the boys. We want them to be smart, intelligent, and brave and self reliant like you. You are selected."

Before I could react, he threw another question at me, "Where will you put up in this city?" And instantly, he was addressing the manager of the school, "Mr. Montgomery, give her the furnished cottage inside the school premises as per her choice. Also look after the other details." Then he looked at me and said, "Miss Durga, you must know that we pay a better package than the government scale. If you work honestly and dedicatedly, enhancing your pay and perks will not be difficult."

The meeting broke off and I saw the Chairman wheeling away. I was left guessing what destiny desired after all.

Young women with throbbing hearts, intuitively sense things likely to happen, at least those concerning their personal lives.

I knew something had happened to me. Something was happening. It was the very first look that we had exchanged. What? How? Why? I did not know. I felt as though the Chairman had taken a part of me along in his big car...on a ride into the unknown.

I was a poor girl. Born and bred in poverty. I knew that loving and being loved was the prerogative of the rich, the prosperous. I had heard enough from many friends how they had been physically assaulted and exploited by their rich boyfriends and then left in lurch, to suffer silently.

Radha had narrated her tale of sorrow in the most mournful tone, "Durga! Do not trust the male sex. They are lustful wanderers. They are all flirts and seduction is in their blood. After their lust is satisfied, they look for some other body, for the sake of variety for the sake of change," she added between sobs. "Man gives love to a woman for sex and woman sex for love.

"The needs of the two work in different directions. There may be a few exceptions. But by and large the rule operates unmistakably."

She had also narrated once the relationship of Rakesh and Meetu, where the man was as steadfast as the mountain and married her despite many hurdles.

Like all philosophers who try to generalise the natural phenomenon, and then become confused to conclude, she said, "Though there are deceptive women as well."

Baffled, I had asked, "Can you say clearly what you want to say? And in case you do not have anything concrete to say, then kindly do not comment?"

"In that case, I would rather like to shut up. What happened with me may not happen with you or others," she had finally concluded.

"It is destiny. You get love and fulfillment by luck and a number of other factors and not because of theories and generalisations about love and sex."

I considered myself unlucky and therefore expected no thrill or fulfillment in life. "Had I been lucky, I would have been born in a different family, different country. I am twenty two. If I had been born in America, I would have had at least led a decent and meaningful life.

Suddenly, Mr. Montgomery asked, "How many rooms do you want to occupy?"

"How many can be given to me?" I asked timidly.

"Madam! The Chairman is especially kind to you. Normally, he does not take interest in the matters of the school. Least of all in the accommodation of the staff," he said sternly.

"You heard the Chairman's orders, that you need to be given an accommodation of your choice," he added.

I could hear the dislike in his voice as he went on, "An employee is either not given any accommodation, or it is as per the directions of the employer and not according to the choice of the employee."

Staring at me through the corners of his spectacles, he said, "He seems to be especially concerned about you. Considering your talents and dedication he has selected you. Please feel free."

The beggars and the poor are alike. If God gives them a chance to ask for anything, they cannot ask for too many things. They will just ask for a new bowl to beg. That really was my case. I thought, 'I should ask for a small room. I can do even without a kitchen. I was thinking how to bring my luggage? I may have to beg money from Sneha to hire some vehicle to transport my luggage. The distance was great. Must be more than 170 kilometers. My luggage consisted of a few things only.'

"Will five rooms, one kitchen and two bath rooms be enough or you want more?" Mr. Montgomery interrupted my thoughts. I guess he wanted to please me so that I could give a good feedback about him to the Chairman, if opportunity came. "Madam! Tell me when you need the services of a truck. It will reach your house to bring your luggage at the management's expense," he concluded.

I wanted to ask if the Chairman had asked to arrange the transport as well for my sake and convenience. But I desisted from doing so, it was somehow against modesty.

I saw the manager extending about 10 five hundred rupee notes to me and said, "Here is an advance of Rs. 5000. You may need the money to shift and all. The worthy Chairman had asked me to give it to you."

I did not know what to do. Why was he so kind to me? Was he like the rest of the men? Did he find me fairly beautiful? What were his intentions? Was he casting a snare for me? While immersed in a pool of delusional thoughts, the manager himself gave me the answer. He said, "The Chairman may come to the school any day, any time. It is his campus. Although it's a rare event, mostly once a year, on his mother's memorial day. I have never seen him visit the school on any other occasion."

The manager dropped me at the bus stand in his car, about 2 km away from school. Before parting, he gave me his mobile number in case I needed any assistance. Sitting on the corner seat in the bus, I was thinking how quickly the circumstances changed. Although, I did not want to think that way, because I was poor, unfortunate and luck never came knocking at the door of our kind. However, the Chairman, Vishal, never left my thoughts. His youthful personality, polite conduct with me and his special consideration for me were enough.

Once again, his looks created an upturn in my mind, I could once again feel the butterflies.

He was a billionaire, educated for more than two years at New York. There was a typical American touch to his personality. He was the sole proprietor of his business empire. Yes, he was 24 and was still unmarried. He was an eligible and lovable bachelor, any girl would vouched for.

But what of that to me?

I am a poor girl, doomed since birth, marriage to him was the wildest imagination for me since I was typically Indian.

For me my chastity, integrity and character held more value than all the wealth in the world. What if he was a millionaire, billionaire or trillionaire!

I did not understand any relation between a man and a woman except only after marriage. 'If he tries to molest my purity, I shall teach him a lesson of life as I did to those four ruffians who wanted to outrage my modesty in the paddy fields.' I thought.

I do not know how they view it out there in the west. There is no doubt being an educated girl I had learnt a lot of the western concepts of live-in relationships, love marriages, contraceptives, pills and the like. But I had not had any romantic opportunity so far although I was 22.

I only knew one thing for sure; men were seductive, lustful and variety loving like any of the male species. It was not only risky but dangerous to have any kind of dealing with them.

Therefore, I resolved not to accept his offer of love or to succumb before his love cravings at all under any circumstances. Ringing in my head again were Montgomery's words, 'The Chairman is especially interested in you and has asked me to personally attend to all your needs, give you good accommodation, transportation and advance.'

'What does all this mean? Is he trying to entrap me in his dark design? I have learnt that the Americans are very sharp. They have invented many advanced devices. The Chairman though an Indian had studied in New York and in the process must have acquired some American traits.

'But I shall be careful not to get caught in his trap and in case he succeeds to an extent, I'll be wary enough to break the trap with the purity of my mind not caring a bit of his being the Chairman or whatever.' I thought.

Out of Vishal's thoughts into the present reality, it was a fact that I had been selected to the Mother India School near Solan, at a handsome salary with good accommodation. I was expected to join the school at the earliest.

I started thinking of the members of my family whom I could get to stay with me at the new place.

My father had been drinking for over decades now. He would leave this world but not his drinks. Bringing him to Solan would be a folly of the greatest magnitude.

My mother would not quit her petty job of working at a number of houses in the colony as help nor would she be spared by them.

My brother! My only dear brother!

Yes. He was the only one. I should help him. I should give him an independent room and let him enjoy the TV and all other amenities. I would cook for the two of us. 'He needs my help.' I thought.

Moreover, the headmaster and the member would not harm the old parents, when I was gone from there. Out of sight would be out of mind.

Jaggi had already been the target of their aggression once and they might pick at him again.

'Yes, it is settled, Jaggi and I will join at my new place of work on Monday; way beyond my earlier school. The transport came. I gathered my luggage and made for the Chairman's Mother India School.'

On the way I overheard the driver of the truck tell his cleaner, "William, she is really very pretty, this new madam! Who will not give his life for her?

"She is a beauty carved by God at leisure while we have been made on contract. The greedy contractor must have hurried with us to get quick money."

"O for a kiss from her!" He added. "Even a touch of her hand can take one to heaven. Just an embrace nothing more..."

"Mind the truck. You are driving on the National Highway number 1. A little negligence will take us to hell," the cleaner remarked mockingly.

The cleaner, who seemed to be an exceptionally wise man further added, "Marriages are made in heaven, celebrated on earth. Man-woman relationships are God gifted irrespective of caste, colour, creed, poverty or prosperity. You and I are the crew of this truck. Let us better mind our work. We should focus at the road that lies in front of us and not at the chiselled faces on the road. You are sure to cause accident."

The driver, took a quick turn on the hilly road and said, "Brother! You are certainly right. Fate controls everything," and thereafter concentrated on his driving.

I did not want to think about the Chairman, yet he never left my mind. I knew he did not pay visits to the school frequently. It was just once a year. Yet I wanted him to come once more, may be just for a while, for my sake.

Since times immemorial novelists have spoken of men besotted by female beauties but here was a different story. A young girl was enchanted by a handsome man, spellbound and zonked.

How eagerly I wanted him to come and meet me or call me anywhere, though thoughts of guarding my honour played simultaneously. A span of six months passed. Everything about the new school was satisfactory. Jaggi was feeling comfortable. He had a lot of space both in and outside the house. My brother and I were well taken care of.

The only thing I kept on thinking about was the Chairman's visit. But he did not come. I kept on waiting, day after day... hope never died.

Suddenly the circumstances took a tremendous turn.

On a very cold night of December 21, I heard a loud bang on my door as if some dacoits had come to loot, plunder and murder. There was a medley of noises, shouts and yelling.

"Durga, open the door. Madam open the door. Chairman has had an accident. It is very serious. Open the door, quick!"

I was at once on my toes and rushed to open the door. I was shocked to know that Vishal's car had been hit by a truck, while he was on his way to the school, and had been badly injured. It was a massive collision and since it was a case of head injury, he had lost his consciousness.

I rushed at the sight and reached out for the manager, "Sir, I have a year's diploma in nursing, let me look after him, till specialised medical help arrives." We quickly got him in the school medical room and throughout I kept the wound on the head tightly pressed.

The manager murmured between sobs, "The Chairman has a golden heart, gem of a man. His life is very important for us, our school, our area and our state. We shall not leave any stone unturned to save his life."

He further detailed, "A helicopter has already left for this place from the Apollo Hospital, New Delhi. It will reach before 4 a.m. I have talked to the trauma specialist at Apollo and he has advised that the loss of blood should be stopped. He was some European doctor and I could not follow his accent.

"Durga, you call him at this number and get the instructions for action at our end till 4 a.m." Accordingly, I called the highly learned European medical man and asked him, "What do we need to do till 4 a.m.?"

"Is the blood flow profuse or slow?"

"Rather very profuse," I replied.

A reply from the other side, "It is a cause to be serious. This means, the patient is passing through the most critical stage." He added, "In that case, can anybody near the patient give him two intravenous injections of the life saving drug, one after the other in just 10 minutes?"

He further instructed, "Don't waste time; if you know how to prick, give him the two injections, quick." He also told me the other details of the first aid and I listened to the instructions very carefully.

Montgomery looked at me puzzled and said, "We are doomed! He is bleeding fast and here in this wintry midnight where do we get a doctor to give him the injections."

He panicked, "Getting the injections will not be a problem, the nearest medical store is round the corner. I know the chemist personally. But who will administer the injections?"

"I can handle Sir, till the time help comes from Apollo. I know how to inject. Rush and bring the life saving injections lest it will be too late."

Montgomery hurried. The Chairman was given the two intravenous injections one after the other. The bleeding slowly ceased.

I did not have a wink of sleep. I asked the other attendants to take a nap as the following day they needed to be full of energy to attend to the patient.

The manager too was on his feet the whole night to check on the Chairman's condition. He had always found me on my toes to assist and serve the Chairman.

The helicopter landed 10 minutes before the scheduled time. When the surgeon Dr. Rupesh Mongha examined the patient, he asked the manager, "Who has nursed him? The initial aid has been so methodical and systematic that the patient now has far better chances of survival. Let the attendant accompany the patient to Delhi."

Montgomery suggested that I should accompany the Chairman to Delhi. He begged, "Will you be kind and accompany us. His life is in your hands."

I was ready to leave in a minute. I was not obliging anyone, but I, for reasons, understood only by hearts that swell with love at the mention of their beloved ones. I requested one of my colleagues to take care of my brother once I was away.

Mr. Montgomery reached Apollo, just when the Chairman was being taken out of the operation theatre. Dr. Rupesh Mongha, warned that the condition of the patient was extremely critical.

"Two major operations have to be performed on the patient, one of which can be taken care of here at Apollo and the second only at New York. If the patient survives both the operations and lives for one month after the second operation, there will be 99% chances of his survival. Till then, nothing can be said with surety. But all this can cost around Rs. 20,00,000 including the expenditure at New York."

He further added,"If you can deposit an advance of Rs. 5,00,000 immediately...," and looked at us.

Mr. Montgomery took out the said amount from a bag. He had brought with him bundles of notes because probably he was an experienced man and knew that the treatment would be a costly affair and there could be no waiting for money. Pay the money and get the relief.

He told the doctor, "Don't bother about the money; the patient's life is very precious. You will get the money in a second and he pointed towards the bag."

The doctor asked the accountant to deal with the formalities and he set off to prepare for the operation.

Mr. Montgomery, looked at me, "Durga, you will probably have to accompany us to New York if there is an emergency. There's no one next of kin to take care of him at this stage."

I did not know how and why, I wanted to go to New York with him. I had prayed to God a thousand times to provide me the opportunity.

When there was a flash of the huge currency notes given as advance, another young woman got ready to go to New York with Vishal. Even her parents wanted to send her with him in case it might click. They wanted to let some intimacy develop between the two which could subsequently be converted into a matrimonial alliance. That would be wonderful!

Even the girl, Sudha like any other young girl, wanted to get a chance to see New York and enjoy the intimacy of a young man who was a very eligible, extremely rich bachelor. They had followed us as soon as they heard of the accident and had already woven their sob story en route. When her mother handed her over a bag containing her clothes and other essential requirements, I felt crestfallen. I thought that all was lost.

I made the last prayer to goddess!

'O kind goddess! Help me. I want to be near him. Goddess! I love him.' I murmured in the weakest of whisper. It was a maiden's confession of my first love. A gentle...soft whisper. God sure listens to the sincere prayers of lovers.

The operation lasted five hours and the gait of Dr. Mongha assured us of the success. It would be two days before the Chairman would be flown to New York, two long days before my fate would be decided. Mr. Montgomery was quiet throughout, as if reasoning who would be the best caretaker for the Chairman.

On the morning of the second day, Dr. Rupesh Mongha, who had seen my devotion, dedication and commitment for the patient came and announced, "The flight to New York is ready. It will have besides the scientific medical machines, three technical operators, including one lady, two doctors, including myself and one attendant for the patient. Make sure that the attendant can speak and understand English most fluently."

Sudha was a class twelve failure. And she had never paid any real attention to the art of communication. She could hardly speak in correct accent of English. The only thing that ever bothered her was her ability to lure men.

Whereas, I had cultivated my communication skills with utmost care and consideration, and could speak English as sophisticatedly as any North American could.

Sudha, at once withdrew. She was hesitant to converse in English and a trip to an English speaking country was altogether nerve wrecking for her. She voluntarily showed her helplessness on the grounds that the weather of New York would not suit her. Besides, she was already continuing here in India with Charan and was almost satisfied with his love and company. It was her third affair and she did not want to fail in it.

When I was the final candidate to accompany the Chairman, Montgomery turned to me, "I am as good as a father to Vishal. I am very happy you are going. I can trust you. I could not trust Sudha or anybody else. I shall look after Jaggi and your family in your absence. Don't bother about the number of days or weeks you are there. Money is of least consideration." He further added, "You are like my daughter! You are no longer a teacher in our group. You are now a personal attendant to the Chairman. Do whatever he wants and keep him pleased when he comes back to himself. Your salary is raised forthwith to Rs. 50000 per month. I shall send you money as and when you need."

Only I know what this opportunity meant for me, money was not my concern, "I will do as you have advised. Only thing I want is no increase in my salary. I am doing it as my duty not for a hike in the salary. I want someone to take care of my brother Jaggi in my absence and my monthly salary be sent to my parents."

As the air craft flew high, higher in the sky, my eyes swelled with tears of gratitude, "O goddess! There is no end to your mercies. Only make me of some service to him in whatever way he likes."

I stole a look at the calm and serene face of the young man, noble, rich and a gentleman...hanging between life and death! Ever since the accident he had not opened his eyes...even once.

I could not take my eyes off his face. His eyes though closed seemed to attract me with a passion inexpressible through words.

✦ ✦ ✦

III

How Much I Love

It was as if even with his closed unconscious eyes, he was constantly looking at me with love stirring the long lost emotions in my feminine heart.

Inviting, irresistibly inviting! O God! Save him for me. I want to love him, embrace him and kiss him unto heaven. Please God do give me this boon of loving him to my heart's content. Please!

That night I shared same space in the aircraft with him. He was physically near me though, he had not spoken a word; I had a sleep full of dreams. Suddenly, the condition of the patient worsened. He needed a unit of fresh blood to be given to him.

I had donated blood so that he could be given blood whenever it was required and there was no shortage. That improved the condition of the patient. The next morning, after a long flight, we landed on the soil of the mightiest country in the world.

The taking off, flying at that height and the landing, all were new experiences for me. In fact everything happening that day was a new...never felt before...never seen before... never heard of either. I even did not mind the jet lag.

But the most surprising and bewildering was the speed of America, culture and progress of the country.

Vishal was at once rushed into the Washington Hospital, one of the best and most credible hospitals in the world. Indeed very costly. But money was in plenty and ready with us.

Two operations needed to be performed. The first operation was quickly planned. It was performed by a set of five surgeons, four Americans and the fifth, an Indian, Dr. Rupesh Mongha who had earned a lot of reputation as a world class surgeon. The operation lasted for 4 hours and 23 minutes.

I was praying all the time. What else could I do?

We had been assured that if the operation turned out to be successful, the patient would start speaking and listening, with healthy vision as before. He would be able to attend phone calls and if the second operation also succeeds, the patient will be able to drive, walk and even run within a month's time.

That night I couldn't sleep at all. I was thinking all the time.

'How would he feel when he sees me so close to him?

'Will Montgomery tell him how I had helped?

'Will he ask me to go back to India, once he comes back to himself?

'Will he like me?'

The operation was over...successfully. The Chairman was shifted to the room and everyone awaited the next morning.

In the morning, I got up quite early, made myself presentable and waited for him to wake up. I went down to the canteen to bring some fresh fruits for him. I also wanted to apprise the manager of the latest developments.

When I called the manager, I found that he was engaged in conversation with someone that lasted for about 10 minutes. When he was free, he was finally connected to me, he said, "It's a miracle, Sir talked to me for 10 minutes.

"I have told him that he survived because of you. I also told him if you hadn't gone out of the way to serve him, he would certainly be no more. You gave him new life. You even gave him your blood." And then he hung up.

With delicate steps, I entered Vishal's room, his eyes were closed. He did not look at me and I did not want to disturb him. May be he had some kind of an attack again.

I went to the doctor's room to check if he was alright. The doctor comforted me, "If the patient has closed his eyes, there is no cause to be panicky. Only thing, he should not have a feeling of nausea nor should he complain of any pain in his head. Give him cold water but only with the help of a spoon, little at a time."

I went to my Chairman's chamber, opened his lips with my comely, delicate fingers as a mother does to her sick child.

I spoke, words saturated with love and passion, "Sir open your mouth a little and take some water. Doctor said you can have some water now." The Chairman obliged like a disciplined baby.

Just then the mobile chimed. The Chairman tried to open his eyes and looked around for his mobile. I picked it up from the side table and gently placed in his hands.

"Hello Montgomery, what news now?"

I could not really understand what they talked. I only saw the Chairman smiling intermittently.

When he was finished with the manager, he turned to me, "Durga, I believe in acknowledging the efforts you made for me. I have learnt from the manager that you served me in every way, even gave me your blood."

He further added,"As Montgomery said, I owe my life to you and I shall never ever forget it." He went on meditatively, "I cannot repay your debt whatever I may do for you and your family. Can you suggest me something that I may do before my second operation. You never know...." Though he didn't speak I knew what he meant.

"Do you need a good car, a bungalow, dollars, gold, diamonds or what?" he continued.

With a gulp in my throat, I spoke, "My family or I don't wish for anything. I have only one prayer if you grant that."

"It is granted before you ask for it. What is it? Tell me what your desire is?"

"Please, let me stay with you till the second operation is over. I shall go of my own accord to my world after you are completely cured. Till then, I shall serve you and pray for you."

The Chairman said something that changed my world forever, "Now your world does not differ from mine. You will always stay next to me, close to my heart and soul."

He reached out for my hand and I felt the warmth in his gentle touch, "I have thought it over. You have created such a space in my heart that no one can fill."

He had hardly spoken these words when he suddenly closed his eyes.

I thought it was a show of emotion or something like that. But when he lay motionless for a while, I panicked and rushed to the doctor's room.

Luckily at that moment Dr. Herbert, the super specialist, who had performed the operation, was there. I told him about the condition of the patient in a special room. After listening to my narration that the patient was in full control of himself for about 10 minutes before passing out, the doctor said jubilantly.

"Congratulations Mrs. Vishal! Your husband is hundred per cent out of danger."

The news was so gladdening and maddening that for a moment I forgot to contradict the doctor, 'Sorry, doctor, I am not the wife of this business tycoon but a mere servant.'

The doctor continued, "Mrs. Vishal, please don't get me wrong. We, Americans are the richest country in the world. We are not mad to earn money. In fact we donate more than any other country in the world, to poor countries for medical help. The fact of the case is that your husband has shown wonderful improvement. At this speed he will totally recover in just 30 days. What I want is that he should get his second surgery done rather early."

"I am extremely happy to know all this. Thank you very much doctor."

I had another question,"Doctor when do you think the next operation should take place?"

The doctor said,"Just in a month. Until then, he will behave most normally. Only thing he will go off occasionally for about 10 to 20 seconds. You will need to follow him like a shadow. Then after the second operation, he will be totally cured. I shall talk to him about it when I come to check on him. If there is a financial problem, we will help in that case.

"Remember one thing only! Do not quarrel with him or lose temper with him at any cost. Keep him pleased! Give him whatever he wants. His mind must be kept at rest, always; he must remain unagitated. Do not deny him anything."

I could clearly understand what he meant by, 'do not deny him anything' although I was unmarried, yet I was young and a sensitive person. I could not make the doctor understand that I could not do anything and everything for him. I was not his wife.

I was a virtuous and pious girl who guarded her honour foremost and would continue doing the same till I got married. When I came back to Vishal's bed, he seemed to be coming back to himself. He called me to his bed, took my hand in his hand, looked into my eyes and said, "Durga! I am really proud of you. You are really a great human being."

Right at that time Dr. Herbert came over, walking towards Vishal's bed with the thoughtful gait, typical of doctors. Noticing us, hand in hand, he smiled as if thinking, "What a blessed married couple! God grant them great pleasures." Doctor told, most politely, the same things to Vishal what he had discussed with me.

He added further, "Mr. Vishal, there is no shortage of competent and highly qualified doctors in India. As a matter of fact many of our American and European patients go to India for treatment. The medical expertise in India is of the same level as that in America. But my contention is that since our first operation has carried off well, I wish to perform the second operation here as well.

"There are two problems, the increased expenses and the personal care. We can give you some concessions if you write an application regarding your inability to bear the expenses. We will almost bring it down to Indian expenditure level.

"So far the question of personal care and an attendant is concerned, I can say with honesty that in my career of 16 years as a doctor, I have never come across a wife looking after and attending on her husband as devotedly and religiously as your wife has been doing. For many nights at a stretch, she did not sleep, did not even wink an eye. I am afraid you may recover and she fall sick!" He added, "I only wish I too had an Indian wife like yours."

Mischievously, he concluded, "Don't tell my wife Susan that I said so, otherwise she will push me out of doors. Winters here in New York are very terrible and killing!"

Vishal was listening with a smile and my heart knew so much joy! "There is no hurry. Still you have one more week to make that decision. I said so because Dr. Rupesh Mongha and I discussed your case at tea and decided that the second operation at this hospital would be ideal."

I prayed to God, "Please God! Let him agree for the second operation at this hospital. It will give me one more month to be near him and serve him." At the same time I was wondering...

'Why do I want to be near him?

'Why do I want to serve him? What is he to me or me to him? What is our relationship?

'I am an Indian woman. I understand that the only relationship between a young man and a young woman other than brother sister relationship is that of a husband and a wife. But a husband wife relationship is established by the due process in accordance to the religion, by observing a number of rituals and other formalities.'

Vishal was again off. He came to himself only after a while. Only the third day, Vishal expressed the desire to go out of the hospital. He wanted to have a look around the city and see how New York as a city, had changed after so many years. It was long back when he came here to study and do his Masters. He wanted to see what changes the new technological advancements had brought in the mega city. He even expressed the desire to eat some fast food.

It was the time of visit of Dr. Herbert. When asked his opinion in the matter, he said, "Mrs. Vishal, it is a very healthy sign. Let him take interest outside himself. The more he goes out the better for his health." He further added, "As for the question of his eating is concerned, you must remember, the trouble is not with his stomach or digestive system or any other system. It is with his head, if at all." He added, "However, you will have to take one precaution."

"What is that?" I asked hurriedly.

"There is nothing to worry at all. But just for the sake of precaution, you will go in the hospital ambulance. In case there is some problem, our driver is not just a driver but a trained professional and has the training required to deal with emergencies."

I felt extremely relieved. I also appreciated the progress of US.

In my life, it was a moment of unprecedented happiness.

'But why after all did I feel happy?' I had no answer to that.

Vishal intervened the flow of my thoughts, "I can't wait to see the city!"

I smiled, "The ambulance will be ready in a while but it will be at our disposal only for a few days. As a precautionary measure, you know. Thereafter you can drive your own car."

Vishal did not create a fuss. He said, "You are great dear. And very quick too!"

I took the Chairman into the wash room with great care, washed his face and cleaned every part of his body, with the help of a warm towel, helped him in putting on his shoes and finally we boarded the ambulance.

The first thing he said in the ambulance, "Don't be worried Durga. I am feeling very comfortable. If there is any problem, I shall at once tell you. Come and sit closer to me."

When I moved in closer to him, he put his hand on my thigh...or was it a sheer chance that his hand came to rest there.

I won't be able to put into words, what I felt. Lofty mountains rotated and the huge gorges turned upside down before my eyes.

'A man's touch on a woman's thigh is not just a touch...it is an expression of his love, his feelings...his mark on the woman that says that she belongs to him!' I felt as if I had been drugged with the strongest formulation of intoxication.

I looked at Vishal, he had closed his eyes as if pretending to sleep. I thought that it was perhaps the safer course. I too closed my eyes in mock sleep. In fact the thrill was benumbing!

The driver of the ambulance, who could see us in the rear view mirror, must have felt strange about us dozing off within minutes of boarding the ambulance.

It was after a span of 5 minutes of trance talked of by the sages, that Vishal opened his eyes and said, "Where would you like to be taken to? Dorris?"

I felt surprised when I was addressed as Dorris instead of Durga and also by the strange question of where I would like to be taken to. I said, "My dear sir, I am not Dorris...I am Durga. I do not know any place in this big and vast city to be visited." "I have changed your name because everything in this country is different from that in India as you will shortly see. I have a request to make, will you please agree?"

"What is that?" I asked. I was overjoyed when the Chairman before whom I was trembling during the interview just eight months back was making a request to me.

"Sometimes what we think may not be right. The other person's view point may be equally right. We should listen to and respect others' point of view and then after thinking logically try to reach a conclusion."

I nodded in agreement.

"Since I have studied here for two years, I shall show you some very interesting places in this Apple City."

He showed me Hotel Times Square, a hotel as though, built not on land but in heaven. I had never seen or imagined a hotel like this, not even in my dreams.

New York Dinner Cruises where if we see the sun rise and sun set in the company of the loved one, we shall feel the bliss of travel to the seventh heaven of delight.

Next day again, Vishal took me to another romantic place of exceeding beauty and charm. Particularly for young lovers, the place was no less than heaven.

Dan Cross Renovations since 1913 have turned Grand Central into more than just a hub for public transport. When the lovers stand there arm in arm, huddled together, it takes them to the wonder land of beauty and charm. Vishal told me that it was both a transit hub and a beautiful example of Beaux-Arts architecture.

Then Vishal took me to Rockefeller Center a great destination for the visitors, located in the midtown Manhattan, Rock Center is probably very famous for its charismatic tree.

Kissing my hand very lovingly, the Chairman whispered, "I wish to pass the rest of my life in your company here under this tree, away from the cares and worries of life and people."

Then he hugged me.

An experience, that could make any maiden forget her morality and reasoning.

Next we went to the Elis Islands and the Staten Ferry. It bewildered me with its charm and bewitched me with its romance. Hand in hand, we walked into the American Museums of Natural History and Vishal showed me the Rose Center Planetarium with its permanent exhibits. Vishal touched my lips rather passionately and I succumbed to his charms. I also returned him a passionate kiss.

After some time we reached the Central Park. From the point of view of a typical orthodox Indian, the park was the gateway to an astoundingly advanced world.

Just at the entry I saw men and women in one another's arms. As I proceeded, I saw couples of all age groups young and old, in teens, in eighties, intertwined like the twigs of the saffron.

A little ahead, I saw, a man and a woman in actual sexual act, lost into another world, unmindful of what was happening around them.

Vishal said, "I will get an ice cream for you."

Although I did not like the idea of eating an ice cream in the icy weather, yet it was a great feeling to see my Chairman run to fetch something for me.

The Chairman was waiting in a queue. In America, you have to stand in a queue for anything and everything and wait for your turn, irrespective of what you are or from where you are or how rich or influential you are!

Suddenly, my attention was attracted to a couple just past the ice cream vendor. They had just begun the game of love making. What the man did to his girl and how she reacted, sensationalised me. Every part of my body was set sensuously aflame.

Through the theory of alternate substitution, I felt drugged. It was not the English wife or beloved who was being caressed or kissed but me. My body was showing some kind of biological thrill and in between, I would feel tremors of a peculiar kind never felt before in life. Vishal was still at number 7. Suddenly, the English couple became peaceful and quiet. What attracted my attention was the love between the two. The desire to love each other was predominant and they were unmindful of their surroundings.

The English lady rested for a couple of minutes with her head on the chest of her friend and then walked up to me. "I have been observing you for some time looking at us intently and lustfully," she said.

"It is insulting to behave like this and disturb the lovers. Staring is bad manners. Don't you have some civic sense in you?"

I apologised, "I am sorry. I am not married yet. Are you married?" I dared to ask.

"No not at all. We love each other and that is all."

She added, "What the hell has marriage to do with love? If two people are in love, the act of sex is sanctified, according to our sexual morality. Marriage without marriage. Otherwise sex is sinful even in marriage. Our sexual morality is based on honesty, integrity, love and mutual faith and cooperation. It is not in being a slave of marriage. We have seen that very often marriage means the end of love. We want love uninhibited."

Just then Vishal came over, holding two cups of delicious ice cream.

The English woman left with her lover, but that short conversation shook my sexual ethics from the very foundations.

Vishal offered the ice cream to me as the Knight at Arms presented a gift to his lady love in fairy tales. I started eating it. While eating, I saw that his eyes were fixed on my face. His deep eyes were searching for happiness and love. I immediately identified what it was and felt a surge of emotions for this man...a sought after person but still so lonely and alone.

Further, I was not a kid now. A short visit to this park had given me much theoretical knowledge. I knew that he had been overwhelmed by my beauty and youth also as I was besotted by his.

After the ice cream was eaten, he took my hand and we went to have a stroll into the beautiful garden. He showed me a number of interesting scenes and sights. In between, we would reach some dark, shady place where an actual drama of sexual union was going on. He would not look at these acts, partly because of coyness and partly because he understood better American code of public conduct.

I would however from the corners of my eyes, unobserved by Vishal, steal a hurried glance and get thrilling sensations.

At one time I was caught unawares and he said to me, "Shoo!!! It is bad manners. Mind your ways."

One can imagine how disgraceful and insulting I, an Indian rustic girl must have felt, when caught viewing a thing like that. It was like a young school girl caught by her father watching a blue movie. After about two hours, he expressed the desire to get back to the hospital room.

When we were coming back, he was lost in the view outside and I too did not feel like disturbing him in the least.

I thought, 'If he would have embraced and kissed me in the park, being fired by what we saw around, would I have opposed it or encouraged his further advances?'

The Indianness inside me surged to give the answer, 'I would certainly have discouraged him. Rather, I would have told him clearly that according to Indian standards anything sexual starts after marriage and not before it under any circumstances. That's what I strongly believe in.'

Vishal and I slept in the same special room provided by the hospital administration that night, yet all went peaceful. Nothing special happened.

I later learnt that doctors kept such patients under heavy sedation. He remained sleeping most of the hours in the night. To be honest, I kept dreaming about him and revisiting the park in my imagination.

Three days later Montgomery came and sought the advice of the Chairman on many important issues concerning business and others. He brought a lot of money also.

Mr. Montgomery was a kind of a man who could not keep any secret to himself and would divulge it out willy-nilly. He said to me, "Madam I feel, one day you will be known as Mrs. Vishal. The Chairman has not told me anything like this but the way he talked about you hinted all the same."

Mr. Montgomery left just in two days because the weather did not suit him. The Chairman did not feel bad when he left. It appeared he wanted to pass most of his time in my company. I did not know why, even I felt good when he left. I felt rather fine to be in the company of the Chairman, alone.

Four days later, after our visit to the Central park, we visited another very romantic place in America, the Empire State Building. There is nothing that can beat the sight from atop the Empire State Building. On a clear day you can see up to a distance of 80 miles. The night time offers the opportunity to see the glamour of the shining city below.

Dorris as I was now called looked at these wonders and Vishal enjoyed it.

I was sipping fruit juice when Vishal asked me, "Dorris, I want to ask you something – something very personal about you. If you don't feel like telling me, you can say 'no' straight way. I shall not feel bad. In fact I love you so much that nothing you do or would do can offend me."

"Sir, please don't talk to me in riddles. Talk straight and I shall give you the answer without concealing anything," I told him.

At once he asked the question that must have been in his heart for long, "How many darlings have you had by now? 2, 3, 5, 8?"

"Sir the fact of the case is that I have had only one darling, in India."

I added, "I fell in love with my darling at the first sight."

Vishal was obviously disturbed but spoke with quite a control over his resentment, "Dorris, you must have thought it strange why did I not get married, being so rich and handsome?"

He continued, "The fact is that I had always wanted to get married to the woman who should meet only one requirement. I want a woman with resistance and character, rather than one who is a saleable commodity. Somebody chaste and good. Somebody who is not ready to give in to lust at the first instance. Poverty or richness of the girl does not matter at all."

With hesitation in his voice he looked straight into my eyes, "Can you forget your darling for my sake?"

"Sir, ours may just be a passing affair in our lives. After you are cured, we will go back to India, to our respective worlds. You to your business and I to my darling.

"Then how can I forget my dear darling, who was my real friend of the bad days of my life?"

At this the Chairman said, "Durga, looking at your beauty, the report about you through Montgomery...of what you did for me and observing your work and conduct here, I had almost decided to marry you."

He held his pocket, "It is a diamond necklace that I wanted to give you as a present here in the Empire State Building for the anticipated marriage. I wanted to make you my bride, my darling and the queen of my heart." He pulled out a very costly necklace and put it back in his pocket. He said politely, "Now let us get going. I shall make a place for you in the first aircraft flying to India tomorrow to attend to your duties. There, Mr. Montgomery will clear your account. He will give you a good sum of money for saving my life, I am not a thankless man.

"I shall also send a nice American suit for your darling and congratulate him from my side for getting the love of a fairy in the person of Durga. I shall pay Rs. 100,000 for your marriage. Besides, I shall buy for your old parents a good house near your parental place, Kalka. I shall also make it a point to come personally to attend your marriage."

"Thank you very much for being so generous and kind to my darling and appreciative of my beauty," I said mockingly. "But if you are really kind and considerate to my darling, please buy a gift that I think will most suit."

"Yes! Obliged as I am to you, all your demands and that of your lover will be fulfilled," said the Chairman in one breath.

My tone was serious now, "In that case buy me one chain cover, one seat cover and two handle covers of the best American quality so that my darling gets a complete makeover."

"Don't talk to me in riddles, Durga." The Chairman's tone was rather impatient.

He said, "Don't stress me out in this condition. Tell me straight what you want and I shall do all the things for you, for as Mr. Montgomery has described you saved my life, before the doctors at Apollo could set to work. I shall always look at you with a deep sense of gratitude."

I was immediately reminded of what the doctor Herbert had said, "Keep him cool and without tension. Give him the moon if he asks for the moon. Do not deny him anything under any circumstances. Not to go cross with him for any reason. That's the easiest and the quickest way to cure him."

I heaved a sigh and smiled, "My honourable Chairman, Sir, my darling is my bicycle." I giggled, "I can give you my brother's number and you can call him and ask about my darling. He will definitely say, it has pined in my absence. Because nobody runs it in my absence. My father unfortunately is a drunkard and my brother Jaggi is differently able. Before joining your school, I used to run it for it saved me a lot of time."

I was enjoying his changed expression, "Since it has been kept out of use, it must have developed many faults, mechanical and otherwise and must look sickly and sad."

Just then, as chance would have it, Jaggi, my brother, called me from India. I handed over the telephone to him to know about the darling cycle.

The Chairman said to the caller, "Durga is okay, she has just gone to the wash room...will call back in a minute."

Hesitating a bit, "Can you tell me the condition of the darling?"

Jaggi spoke from the other side, "Tell her that I was worried about her. The condition of her darling cycle is as bad as anything. If she allows me I shall sell it for whatever it can fetch from Rs. 80 to 100 later on, it would be hard to sell it at all."

When I received the message from my brother, through the Chairman, with news from home, I was happy.

I immediately called my brother back and said, "First go to the goddess in the temple. Thank her for giving me my darling. Then sell it for just Rs. 25 and not a penny more. Before selling it off, do tell the buyer the inner secret. If he wants to talk to me let him speak to me."

The Chairman was at once convinced beyond doubt that the darling was nobody else but the bicycle. He said after I hung up, "Dorris! I am extremely repentant. I am ashamed. I am regretful. I beg from you a hundred thousand apologies."

"None of these things. Don't tax yourself. For I have told my brother to sell off my darling of the younger days." I told him I would tell him the story of my darling back in the hospital.

In the ambulance, I felt that the Chairman's hand once again on my thigh, as he said, "Dorris! I once again am sorry, extremely sorry!"

I most politely, submissively and lightheartedly said, "I find you a fickle minded man. In last 30 minutes you have four times addressed me as Durga and two times as Dorris. What do I understand? Am I Durga or Dorris?"

"Yes! You are right. Since, you said you have a dear darling and with whom you would yet like to carry on, I was shaken up. Though I stayed in America for two years, I cannot shed off my Indian roots completely."

I said, "Sir I feel proud of your love and regard for your Indian roots."

At this Vishal said, "All cultures in the world have some good and bad points. But none of the points is exclusively negative. Everything is the product of environment, and cultural background dependent on many factors. All is okay because God has made all. Science can go wrong, God cannot. God is great and supreme. America, to be sure, possesses one of the best standards of culture and civilisation. It is a harmonious mixture of multicultural, multi-ethnicity and multiple languages."

That night as the two of us were tired, we fell asleep just after 10 p.m. At about midnight, I felt somebody had tried to touch my body. I got conscious.

I saw Vishal by my side, his hand on my back. I did not know if it was by chance or a deliberate attempt by the him.

I started getting a sensation, a sensation felt only in youth by the touch of a person you love, and the touch you so much crave for. I started perspiring from head to foot. In the chilly wintry night, that part of my body which came under the influence of his touch seemed to be giving out fire.

I could have pulled my body from under the arm and left it dangling. But that I did not want to do. I could not do. I was not willing to. I confess, a unique pleasure felt only by a lass rushed from head to foot in my body.

After sometime, he himself withdrew the arm and I felt bad.

Suddenly the scene of the Central Park where a woman loved a man rather ferociously came before my mind's eyes and I felt like slipping into Vishal's bed. Marriage without marriage!

It was after lot of efforts that I could calm my warmed up body.

I was sure that one day, bodies would win and my Indian morality would not be able to help. When only two days were left for the final major operation Vishal took me to Brooklyn Promenade, a very romantic place in NY, a place often visited by couples married or unmarried to celebrate their honey mooning. It also offers the visitors a spectacular view of lower Manhattan. There is a famous River Café where the rich took their beloveds to get pleasure and see glamour.

✦ ✦ ✦

IV

The Stolen Bicycle

I was as intoxicated as a man on drinking a full bottle of Vat 69. It gave me perfect pleasure to enjoy the heavenly delicious chocolate at the Jacques Torres Chocolate Shop.

Back in the room, Vishal seemed to be in a very happy mood. He asked me the first thing, "Dorris why did you call your bicycle as darling?"

I said, "Sir as I have told you a couple of times before also, I belong to a very poor family. My father, though a qualified engineer became an alcoholic. He would either earn no money, or if he did earn anything; he would drink it away and would not give any penny towards family expenditure. My brother Jaggi is polio affected. I wanted to buy a cycle to go to the college which was 10 miles away from my house. All cycles were very costly. Second hand, third hand and even tenth hand cycles were beyond my power to buy. I could spend only Rs. 40 at best. Then came this cycle. I subsequently christened it darling."

I further added, "One of the teachers bought a new cycle. He had this old cycle spare with him. I approached him and requested, 'I am very poor. I do not have a cycle to ride to the college. If you could give me yours I shall never forget your kindness.'

This world is full of generous and kind hearted people. He at once said, "You need the bicycle very badly, I can understand you cannot buy a new one. Okay! Take the cycle from my house. I paid only Rs. 25 for it and I will get the same amount. When you sell it, sell for the same amount.

"He added further, 'Only thing, it is a stolen cycle. The person who sold it to me had only later on told me so. I was never questioned by the police. Hopefully you will also not be checked but in case you, you must not take my name. If you agree you can come and take it right way.'

"I gratefully acknowledged his gesture, Sir, beggars are not choosers.

"I went to his house and paid the said amount, gave alms worth Rs. 5 to the poor and brought it home.

"I knew I could buy only a stolen cycle.

"As I mounted it for the first time I requested it, 'Darling my safety is your responsibility. To possess you, I have paid a very heavy price. I have taken the law in my hands. And like a true lover it has so far protected me.'

"Tell me sir, do I commit a mistake if I call it darling and love it like one?"

There were tears in the eyes of the Chairman, he said, "There is so much misery in this world, and I can do so very little."

"I assure you that I will always love you, care for you and protect you." Saying so he extended his arms towards me and invitingly asked me, "Day after is my operation. It is a major operation. Let the doctors say what they will. It can cause death. It can prove fatal. Will you allow me to love a fairy, the most beautiful woman of this world for a while?" He repeated in whispers, "For a very short time before death!"

I thought, 'He is inviting most yearningly. He is craving for my companionship. He wants to love me completely. The English woman said love is the only criterion, not marriage.'

I searched my consciousness for an answer: Do I like him enough? Do I love him enough? Will I be to him what Eve was to Adam? Should I show him how a woman complements the man? How a man is just so incomplete without a woman?

I found every part of my body was melting to be one with his. I loved him tremendously.

But I had my principles! I had my sexual ethics. The Indian ethics!

I did not condone any relation between man and woman of the sexual kind under any circumstances...unless they are married.

'No, I shall not go to his bed. If once I go, it will be all gone through. Oh God! What a difficult choice. I want to go and I do not want to go. No, I shall not go at any cost.'

I thought, 'I may be shunted back to India, if I deny. He is my employer. He is my pay master. He can do anything. He can even use force.'

I further thought, 'My services may be terminated.

'But no, no.

'He may be a very rich eligible bachelor!

'For me my virtue and chastity was the richest thing on earth!

'A person's virtue is far more precious than all the kingdoms of the world.

'He says, he is sick, and may die during the operation.

'It is true. Most neurological surgeries are fatal.

'It is a sin to deny the last wish of an ailing man. Even the convicts condemned for hanging are not denied it.'

All the arguments were in favour of sleeping with him for one night, the last night of his life. Above all to be honest, I myself wanted it.

Vishal said, "Come Dorris come. I cannot breathe without you," He said and waited for me.

He was sure that the woman who had served him like a dutiful wife could not deny the pleasure of a night, his handsome body, his being the only son and sole heir to a grand property!

The hospital authorities as usual, switched off the lights at 9 p.m. so that the patients could relax undisturbed.

I closed my eyes. I controlled my passion. I closed the doors of my heart to the assured anticipated thrill. I ignored my career and decided.

'No, not at all. At no cost without marriage.'

I thought, being tired and exhausted of the day's fatigue, he would also sleep after a short while.

I closed my eyes and pretended to sleep.

Vishal kept on searching me with the search light of his eyes and requesting me time and again not to deny the last wish of a sick man.

I thought, 'Sex with me is not ambrosia that will save his life, if he is fated to die! Sleeping with me will not, cannot, snatch him from death if he has to die. No, for me, my purity is more precious than any act of charity, divinity or mercy! Even his living or dying! I am an Indian girl and I will uphold my integrity.'

I did not count, probably, he called me about 28 times to come to his bed. I ignored and did not respond. I turned my face and tried to sleep.

Venerable! Respectful!

Adorable! Lovable!

Goddess showered her blessings in the form of sleep and I fell into the lap of slumber. Vishal told me later on that he kept on calling me again and again till 10 p.m.

At 10 p.m. Vishal called my name rather very loudly and I sprang on to my feet thinking as if something unusual had happened.

Vishal being my Chairman, my officer, my employer and my boss, I could not deny him anything except my honour. Moreover in the hospital, I was his employee and had been called here to be serviceable to him, and assist him; sick as he was.

I said most respectfully, "Yes Sir! Do you need anything? Can I do anything for you?"

He said, "You can do a lot for me, if you please." He looked piteously at me. He asked me to open his very personal brief case. He gave me the keys to open it. It was a brief case of a very rich man and no employee, not even the manager; Mr. Montgomery was suppose to touch it, leave alone opening it. It contained the Chairman's very personal documents.

"Should I open it sir?" I asked to be certain.

"Yes! Open it, take out the legal papers lying at the top and read those aloud."

Though I was tired and wanted to sleep, I had no option but to open it, take out the papers and read aloud what was written on those. I was happy to see the dictation; it did not run into many pages but only a few lines. It read: 'If my operation of 23rd October fails and I happen to die, all my properties be divided as per my will. None of my relatives be given anything out of my property. They are all selfish and did not help me when I was in need.

A sum of one lac be given to each of my servants who served me. Montgomery being an honest and kind person should be given Rs. 10 lakhs. Besides, both his daughters are to be married off with funds from my account. Montgomery will look into it.

My total money, accounts, property, movable and immovable be given to my wife, Mrs. Durga Chadda whom I married in New York. I put on my mother's ring on her middle finger as a testimony of the fact that I married her and signature in the presence of my Attorney Beaforson, in the presence of the judge, Mr. Davidson of the Matrimonial Court, New York.'

The Chairman had got all that done through the manager when I went to pray for him in the nearby temple.

It was all that was written and that was to be read.

Vishal held a very costly ring worth perhaps millions of rupees and asked for my hand.

I refused to extend my finger or to become his wife like this. Tears in my eyes, I said, "Sorry Sir, I am neither interested in your property nor in your money. I am an Indian girl and I value my character and purity above everything else. I am going to tear out these papers. I can become your wife after you marry me in a proper way either at a temple or in the court of law in the presence of hundreds of friends, well wishers and relatives. I do not like this marriage without marriage.

"It is only then that I shall put on your ring and sleep with you as a wife. Till then, please, excuse me. You do not know how much I love you but I love my principles more. I will have any physical union with you only after marriage in a proper way. Not like this!"

Quiet disheartened Vishal put the papers back along with the ring. He said soberly, "Okay, Durga! I shall wait till the operation is over, by the end of this week only."

"Yes! Vishal! I can better be won over by love rather than these legal papers or lure of money." I turned my face and again the goddess of slumber was gracious to accept me into her lap after some time.

Shortly before mid night, I felt a hand on my body, moving gently and caressing me. I at once became conscious.

Vishal had come near me. I asked most politely and submissively, "Sir what do you now want? What can I do? Please go off to sleep.

"Please try to sleep.

"Please sleep.

"Please.

"Pleas...

"Plea..."

His touch intoxicated me so much that I began to fumble. Suddenly, I did not know what happened to me, my body, me and my soul. Everything seemed to be revolting against me. It became responsive to his caressing and the erotic passion thus aroused. Long drawn kisses, warm cosy embraces followed. It dissolved my resolution.

There, there it flew to Cupid!

All my determination not to yield under any circumstances, evaporated.

'Oh! God! What is this happening to me,' I thought. My own body was not in my control any longer now. It understood no command of logic. It just swayed to yield to Vishal's youth. I no longer remained I. My whole self was electrified into romance, passion and desire. I was now not Durga or Dorris. I was passion, pure and simple and uncontrollable!

God has put very strange, powerful magic into the male touch. It can set a woman's body aflame. It can make her red hot like burnished brass.

My senses stopped working. I was drugged into a forgetful oblivion. Every system of restrain and control failed. I was melting. It was passion throughout.

I did not at all want to do it for the entire wealth of the world. But under the forceful impact of Vishal's youth, I was more than willing. Instead of pushing him away, I was pulling him to myself.

Like Yeats' Leda and Swan.

Yes! Pulling...continuously in a rhythm that I had never experienced before. The lightning flashed and the clouds thundered in the sky. Here on the hospital bed, our passion surged hard, dissolving us together, taking from me, my well guarded virginity.

Vishal and I were holding each other in a tight embrace.

Utter trance!

Total canonisation.

A little later, our breathing normalised and eyes refused to open.

We both fell asleep, in each other's arms, closely throbbing hearts. It was Vishal who woke up first, at about 4 a.m. He felt extremely repentant at what had happened the previous night. In fact when he came to my bed, he just wanted to express his love through his body language which he had already done in so many words.

By a few sweet hugs at best and nothing more.

By the exchange of a couple of honeyed kisses and nothing more.

By a few more sensuous steps of love.

Certainly nothing more than that!

But what had he done in spite of trying to stop himself. Not he, but his body had done it.

The union of two young bodies had done it. The wise people are right when they say: a young couple is like oil and a match stick, they can catch fire any time.

He thought, 'How shall I show my face to Durga for forcing her to do what she had refused to do at the cost of my total property? I am guilty. I must beg pardon from her. I will catch her feet and will not leave those, till I assure her that I shall not do any of those things before marriage under any circumstances again.

'I shall shoot myself with the revolver I bought from Paris for my protection if I ever do it, however enchantingly thrilling it might have been. I must beg a written apology from her for spoiling her purity which she valued above everything else in this world.'

He got off the bed, opened his personal briefcase yet again and on one of the stamp papers he wrote the following few lines.

'I am sorry that I spoiled your purity, this night of 22nd, in room number 11 of the American Washington Hospital much against your wish. I promise you that just after the operation tomorrow, I shall marry you, Durga and then like a hero stand by your side, forever! Signed in the presence of God and swearing by my dead mother, yours, and only yours forever. Wait for just a few days more, please. Vishal.'

He secretly hid the document beneath my clothes in the bag, while I was still asleep and then came to my feet. He held my feet with both his hands. I immediately woke up. I did not want to talk to him for what he had done with me. I held him totally responsible for what had happened. He should not have come so close. He was an ailing man and should have stuck to his bed.

But, in my heart of hearts, I knew I was equally responsible. All the parts of my body had started dancing as passionately as a peacock dances in the gardens when it sees its mate. Like a she squirrel acts before a he squirrel, when in heat. I had become infatuated at his touch. But I would never again allow him to repeat it under any circumstances.

I felt his tears falling on my feet. I felt belittled. My Chairman weeping! My beloved weeping for a fault both of us were to be blamed for!

I, however, was a little more at fault. If I did not allow the weak moment to take the over me, it would have never happened. It could not have happened.

Instinctively, and most impulsively, I bent down towards him, pulled him on my bed, just to soothe and console him...it was destiny that wanted it to be so and was the fault of neither of us.

And I had intended to make it clear to him that I, in my senses, would not allow any repetition of the same act.

My heart ached to see the tear drops on his cheeks and I held myself responsible for them and kissed the most precious pearls, wiping them.

Suddenly, we found ourselves kissing each other most passionately. A kiss, initiated to regret the mistake we mutually made. But it was a kiss that took both of us to Keatsian magic casements opening on the foam of forlorn fairy lands! Neither of us remained in our senses any longer.

The resolve of not repeating the act ever in our senses, vanished in thin air. It ended with another passionate encounter – an act both of us had so solemnly decided to avoid.

It just happened.

Angels must have laughed at Cupid's play once again. So engrossed we were in the act, that we failed to take notice of the young nurse who had come for the routine morning check up. She quietly slipped out of the room. A second later we were stirred by a knock at the door. It was the voice of the same nurse, 'The Chief Doctor is on a visit, hope you are ready.'

We exchanged a glance and giggled. Surprisingly, the whole afternoon there were no more visits to our room. Time flew by without us taking notice of the hours.

The hospital staff did not disturb us either. The foggy windows were, I guess, only stood witness to the encounters inside.

May be they wanted the patient and the attendant to relax before the major operation.

Four o'clock, we received a call from the reception, Montgomery had come from India.

Sudha was still not out of the field. It was rumoured in the whole of Solan district that she had secretly run away with her fiancé no. 4, Sunny Sharma for a period of one week and had just come back the day before. Once again deciding what a misfit her fiancé was for her. Immediately her mother sent her to New York, to try her luck once again, a rich prospective husband, more a choice of her mother than a liking of her own. She was neither properly educated nor beautiful.

But God had definitely made everyone in pairs to continue life on earth.

Vishal did not like her presence, he knew that she was not only ugly from outside, but uglier from inside.

Vishal did not have many relatives. The few that were there were most selfish and wicked. They had deceived him in times of need. Some of them, the closer relatives had tried to harm his interest grievously or hit him physically. His only confidant was Montgomery.

He called him into his room and sat closely huddled with him for about one hour.

'It has been rather a long time,' Sudha thought.

"He must be giving him details regarding his business," I replied.

Inside the room, Vishal told Montgomery, "Please, open the brief case and take out the legal papers. Put your signature, there. Everything else is taken care of. This briefcase will remain with you. It contains my wishes, my will and everything that belong to me."

He added, "I am throwing the key out of the window into the wilderness. Nobody should open it. Not even you. If I come out safe and sound from the hospital, I shall open it. If I die, there, in the operation, you will break it open and do accordingly. Finally, remember, that I love Durga as a wife. Give her all protection and care in my absence like you would to my wife and your child. Do you understand?"

Without another word, the briefcase came into Montgomery's coveted possession.

Sudha was eyeing everything with suspicion. But she was looking at Durga most contemptuously. Vishal hated the very sight of Sudha. Just before going into the operation theatre, he said to Montgomery, "I am leaving my wife Durga in your protection and care. I should be in my senses in three or four days, if all goes well. But if luck is against, you will please protect Durga against all odds. The worst of the odds is Sudha and her mother."

He called me and said, "Durga darling! I am not a cheat. I remember whatever you have done for me. If I remain alive, my life will always be yours."

He left without looking at anybody else, for the operation theatre. In fact none belonged to him as dearly as I. The operation was supposed to take not more than one hour. But it took eight hours.

Doctors were not commenting on the status of the operation. It is medical ethics, not to tell the relatives immediately of anything unpleasant.

But truth has to be told. It cannot be kept a secret for long!

Finally, Dr. Rupesh Mongha told the sad news for all but a happy one for Sudha and her mother, "The operation, was quiet risky. It was with great difficulty that he has been saved but I fear that he might lose his memory. He might wake up unmindful of his own self, his name, or his occupation.

"He will also forget of his old acquaintances, friends and relatives and all the incidents that took place in his life in the past. He will however remember everything here from. According to Ayurveda, such patients do come back and remember their past, one day, but that we cannot say. It is only when God wants it or something unusual happens in their lives."

For Durga and Montgomery, all was lost!

For Sudha and her mother it was a mighty opportunity and a great beginning. Sudha would get a chance to develop intimacy with Vishal. They were already planning, "Fix him hard on the first day of your meeting. Make him Sudha addict. Then everything will follow. I was only a prostitute's daughter. This is how I hooked your father, a rich man then. My mother told and taught this great trick of dealing and winning males. It is with tricks that men are won. And the woman's greatest trick, her trump card is her sexual appeal and how best she makes use of it. Good Luck! I will so arrange that Durga is not allowed to sleep near him. You will sleep near him, the whole night and rest you know. You are pretty experienced. You have already had four lovers.

"But be careful, like every shrewd woman, you must do what you want to do but make it look that he did it and forced you also into doing it. You may use force but he must be made to feel that it is he who used force.

"To make the matters foolproof, Sudha, you put sleeping tablets in Durga's tea. She wouldn't stand the strength of the sleep inducing tablets, and would fall asleep on the nearest sofa."

Sudha's mother commented, "Poor Durga! She must have been so tired after all these nights of care taking. She is a great girl. I always wish the best about her. It is a critical time though. I have decided that Sudha will now onwards look after the Chairman. We are relatives. We know how to care for Vishal most properly."

While, her mother was so maneuvering, Sudha was smarting up for the night encounter, using perfumes, powders, puffs and oil and a large variety of other sex aids under her professional mother's advice. Little did she know...

'Beauties in vain their pretty eyes may roll, charms strike the sight but merit wins the soul.'

Right then, Dr. Herbert, the chief Surgeon said to Montgomery, "No female under any condition, sleep near him or in the same room. It can kill the patient because of exertion, it is most important. The hospital ward boy, Robert will sleep in his room and look after him for at least four days and then according to the condition of the patient; you can fly him carefully to India."

From a corner in the ward, the nurses exchanged mischievous glances. They had known the two blossoming flowers in love. They did not want the ugly vampire Sudha to share what belonged to Durga and her devotion for the sick man.

It appeared, one of them had told the chief surgeon what she had witnessed between the two lovers. Dr. Herbert did not want the sick man to make any kind of exertion.

He was a very experienced doctor. He knew how to handle the situation and the sick man.

Sudha on the other hand looked as a picture of pity and misery. All her efforts to make herself look charming and attractive were ending in vain until she found Spenser, another ward boy, eyeing her seductively. That night, she had to rest contented with Spenser as a lover.

It was after four days that Vishal came to consciousness. But as was feared, he had forgotten everything that happened in his life prior to the second operation.

He would particularly look at Durga as if he did not know her at all and was trying to remember something concerning her. But nothing concrete would come in his mind.

Sudha had liked Spenser, the Englishman, like anything. She wanted to discuss back home in India about her new found lover with her friends. Spenser took Sudha around all the romantic places in the city. Without telling her mother, Sudha married Spenser secretly and believed that the dream of her life had been realised.

When her mother came to know of her daughter's nasty and hurried decision, she was taken over by depression. She wanted her to hook Vishal as a husband for her daughter, by all means. She had forgotten that much above her planning was the planning of God.

After a fortnight all were on the aeroplane.

Sick Vishal.

Depressed and shattered Durga.

Sudha in a corner of the plane confided to her mother, "I have become sick of him. It is because of language problem. Except the language of sex, we cannot understand anything. My English is very bad. I failed four times in class twelve. I cannot live with him anymore. I promise now I will try to get Vishal as a husband. He is very rich. I will hook him the way you hooked my father! I did not tell anybody that I married secretly in New York."

God has made all kinds of humans. Here was Sudha and there was Durga!

Poles apart!

The plane landed at the Indira Gandhi International Airport. All the members had their separate and specific planning. Montgomery had reached the airport in a big car to receive Vishal. He had also made arrangements for me and Sudha in the same car. Montgomery himself was driving the car.

But Vishal in the car behaved most strangely. He did not recognise any body including the manager, Montgomery. In the car, Vishal asked Montgomery, "Who am I? Where do I belong to? Where am I being taken?"

Furthermore, he wanted to be introduced to the rest of the occupants of the car.

It was clear that Vishal had forgotten all about his past life, everything before the operation. He was a blank notebook and everything had to be written anew and started afresh.

The only wonderful thing was or at least it so seemed, he still and so far had been talking to Montgomery only in English. His hold on the language being so chaste and elegant, it had continued to be so and was a point of surprise for all those who knew him.

Montgomery took the initiative and told Vishal that he was a very rich man, an owner of a number of industries. His headquarter was at Solan, in the mountains. Solan was a hilly, romantic place on the road between Chandigarh and Shimla. His father was a very wise man. He had built the business empire for him. He had a special love for the hills, its climate and its scenic beauty, its rivers and its sky kissing mountains.

Then he also explained the number of industries and factories owned by him throughout India.

Both his parents had died and he was always betrayed by his relatives whom he did not trust any longer.

Suddenly, Sudha asked Montgomery to stop the car as she was interested in taking a corn cob which was being prepared on a wayside stall, over in the soft burning flames.

She got off the car, crossed the road and stood bargaining for a petty amount.

"Who is this ugly lady? What does she want with us and why she is not asked to go out of the car?" were a volley of questions Vishal asked Montgomery.

Montgomery had a grouse against this girl or lady or what?

She had tried to stand in way of Durga. She had insulted Montgomery on a number of occasions. She was always rude to elders. In fact, to insult others, gave her a sadistic pleasure.

All this she did under the cover of being a relative of the Chairman's family which in fact, she was not. Introducing her, he told Vishal that she claimed to be his distant relative. Her mother was still more vicious than her and she had an eye on his property and wanted to hook him as a husband, knowing well that in a neurological surgery he lost his memory.

Vishal asked in a rather hushed voice. "Who is this paragon of beauty, sitting at the back seat?"

Montgomery was a real American and like all Americans was honest to the core and would give his life to speak the truth under all circumstances.

He said, "Honourable Sir, she was your sweetheart before you went into oblivion and forgetful state. It is she who gave her blood to save your life, who served you as the most cherished beloved does for her lover and nursed you as a mother nurses her incapacitated son. You had the most special love and consideration for her and expressed your desire to marry her and her alone."

He added, "You also requested me to be very careful with her and watch her interests after the operation. You asked me to protect her as your wife, your most loved companion.

"She richly deserves to be given all the care and consideration. Please stand by my previous orders in her case. What is her name and what does she do?" Vishal unbelievingly replied.

Montgomery said, "Sir, she is a teacher in our school and has an accommodation given to her by you, inside the campus."

"It is fine; I shall like to visit her someday," replied Vishal.

All this time, I was pretending to be sleeping in the car.

God had been so gracious that the fire in the oven on the hilly road did not brighten so Sudha stood outside; and my total case had been discussed by the Prince of my dreams.

He became impatient like the true master of the group of industries and said, "Fuck her on the road itself and let us get going."

I felt happy to hear, "I shall visit her accommodation some day."

I said to myself, 'I shall wait till eternity for that day.'

By now, Sudha, the vampire walked back into the car scheming to destroy me from the roots, knowing little that the Protecting Providence can control all the devils of hell like Mephistopheles with all their dark designs.

"And who are you?" Vishal asked.

"I am Montgomery. You had appointed me as your Manager. Besides, you trusted me in everything. You can, please maintain your faith and trust in me and I assure that I shall remain absolutely faithful to you in future as I have been in the past."

Montgomery further added, "Sir, since you have just been relieved from the hospital, you look so much tired and weakened. I understand the business from all angles. If I need anything, I shall seek your advice otherwise can I go ahead with the running of business if only you put your trust and faith in me."

Vishal's response was rather quick, "Montgomery, this is wonderful. I feel tired and exhausted," and added, "You look after the business as you have been doing in the past. But remember, don't break anybody's heart by any misconduct with the employees."

I was still pretending as if I was sleeping but thinking, 'Even in his unhinged condition, he is still great and lovable. My lovable darling, Vishal.'

"First of all just let me have a look at all my factories and establishments. How much time will it take?" Vishal commanded.

"Only four weeks," replied Montgomery.

"Will it be tiring? Uncomfortable? Where will we stay?" Vishal asked in a lost tone.

"It will not at all be tiring. We have our own rest houses in each establishment and I will get all of these fixed up before we reach there," replied Montgomery.

"Okay. You are great Montgomery," said Vishal and dozed off.

The whole scene of room number 11 on the night of the 22nd flashed in my consciousness. I was not only romanticised but mesmerised too.

I came back to the school and set on my duties as a teacher. There was much to be done with the students. Their academics as well as the cultural activities of the school had to be properly attended to.

Besides, I had not forgotten the incident with the four ruffians in the paddy fields near the foothills. It was my deftness in the art of Judo that had helped me to protect my honour and save my chastity at the hands of those four ruffians. I wanted to train all willing girls of the Mother India School in the technique.

Moreover, the worthy Chairman had appointed me specifically for this purpose. Though the Chairman had forgotten me because of the changed circumstances. It was my misfortune that the operation did not come out completely successful, otherwise the situation today would have been totally different and heavenly.

It was on the way from New Delhi to Solan that Sudha had felt a change in the behaviour of the Chairman. It was true that she had never ever been paid any attention by Vishal at any stage. It was also true that she had had relationships with about a dozen men both, Indian and American.

But God has assigned each human being a mission in his or her life.

✦ ✦ ✦

V

Love in America

She had married Spenser in New York and had deserted him, in a way. She had come back to India, so much so, without telling him where she was leaving for.

The night before leaving for India, she had asked Spenser in her own way, "Darling! You love me...do you...yes...tell how much?"

And Spenser had replied, "Sudha, yes I love you and I love you true as tax."

Sudha was surprised and did not know what tax had to do with love.

May be in America even love was taxed. Spenser meant to say that honest tax payers had to pay tax in everything; his was true in his relationship.

She then asked, "You sleep women how many I before?"

Spenser replied, "We Americans are probably the best lovers in the world. Firstly, we do not count how many men or women we come in contact with. Secondly, our views about love and sex are very liberal and rational. Of all we are not cheats or hypocrites like people around the world. We believe in honest dealings and we care a lot for the female sex."

He further added, "In fact we hold women in high respect to the level of adoring them. We hate what you call a double standard of morality. We do not have a sexual code of conduct for men and a separate one for the women. We do want purity and chastity in sexual unions. But for us much more important than the physical purity is the purity of the heart, mind and soul."

He went on, "A man, as also a woman, can commit infidelity under circumstances beyond control. In that case he or she cannot be ostracised. We condemn the prostitutes of the mind, as really damned souls. We do not keep the feminine gender under force and threat. The use of physical violence is unimaginable in our country. Man-woman relation is a gift of Gods to mankind. They must enjoy the honeyed rhythm and the melodious harmonies that come out of this relationship, feel the ecstatic thrill and passionate intimacy, the supreme bliss of divinity rather than attacking the dignity of the relationship through parochial considerations and outdated, meaningless taboos."

Sudha could not make either head or tail of what her husband was saying.

She therefore said to him, "I not understand...you speak what...decision...wrong my...stupid I was...marriage only... same country...others may play with."

She asked a straight question again and requested him to for a straight reply, "Women have you come across...how many...before meeting me? Me good than others...what my number?"

"You are my fifth true love. The earlier women I met were all flirts." Spenser asked her in the same vein, "And where do you place me in the same question?"

"You are first, the only one! I never...I will never with a man other than you." she lied to him quite professionally.

"Great! Wow! What great Indian sexual purity! Do you think I trust what you say?"

Heart of hearts, he knew that no doubt Indian sexual morality is really laudable, but in Sudha's case, she was telling a lie. He knew that she was an exception and not a true model of Indian feminine morality. Durga stood for true Indian feminine character.

Although, Sudha's number of sexual encounters was one more than his, but she forgot about her own misdemeanours. Like many other self proclaimed, moralists, she kept on thinking about his being unfaithful and a flirt and finally deeply regretted having married him in the court of law.

Next day, when Spenser came to his Indian wife's bedside to tell her that she was really a great girl and he loved her truly, he found her bed empty. The cage was there but the bird had flown across seven seas in search of pastures new and enchantments eastern in the entourage of the Chairman and others.

She was quite a secretive girl and did not tell anyone that she had married Spenser in a federal court of law in America. She pretended that she came a virgin to America and went a virgin to India, minor encounters in youth were accidental and irrelevant.

Sudha was still optimistic though Vishal had not taken any notice of her whatsoever.

I was optimistic because Vishal had spoken approvingly of my beauty and charm to Montgomery. Montgomery, the noble soul was also optimistic because Vishal was showing some positive attitude. Geeta, Sudha's mother was a shrewd dancer and did not accept defeat; only thought that it was one of the performances that did not go as best as she had expected. She was optimistic that I being out of the arena, her daughter had all the chances of success if Sudha danced with rhythm and melody.

Sunny Sharma, the boy with whom, Sudha had eloped for a week had liked her company best because she had spent a lot of her mother's money on him. He was given to drinking and womanising at the willing woman's cost. He was optimistic when he learnt that she still was single and was now willing to marry her if the necessity arose.

Back home, she found that her mother Geeta was still bent upon hooking onto Vishal as a husband for her.

She told her, "Sudha! I have lived in this world for a much longer time than you. I have already experienced the coldness of this world with you in my womb. Remember, there is always a chance to succeed in this world, only if you want to succeed and still more if you know how to succeed."

She advised, "Men are generally the least dependable in this world. They live by the sole premise that, any and every woman is beautiful when the candle is off."

The illiterate mother advised with a rather literary metaphor, "Sudha, always remember the story of King Bruce and the Spider, and try, try again."

Sudha was quiet irked, "Mother, man woman relationships are neither a battle ground nor a winning and losing match."

She immediately retorted, "It is purely a battle of sexes."

Looking at the disgust on her mother's face, she sobered, "Okay mother, I shall try."

Though she was sure that she hardly had any chance with Vishal who was intentionally avoiding her and she could read the utter disgust on his face when she happened to appear before him.

Strange are the ways of God. Montgomery did not know that Vishal had made a will and that the will was in the brief case which he still had in his possession. According to the will, he was to get huge funds from Vishal's accounts to marry both his daughters. But he was to tear open the brief case in the eventuality of Vishal's death not before. Vishal was very much alive but he was no longer the old Vishal but a different person altogether.

The only person who knew all the secrets of the briefcase was I. I had read the will completely and attentively. I clearly remembered the total content line by line. But I loved Vishal now very dearly after what had passed between the two of us, despite ourselves. Therefore, I did not want to make any reference to the contents of the briefcase to anybody at all.

Besides I had already read the stamp paper which Vishal had hidden beneath my clothes. In the eyes of law it was a speaking confession of Vishal about everything that happened on the night of 22nd. But I did not want to get his love by a decree of the court of law.

I wanted to hug him unceasingly and wanted him as my dear loving husband!

I had full faith in divine retribution. I knew that sooner or later, one day, God's mercies would come and then there would be shower of love, romance and trance. I was prepared to wait not only in this life but as per the Indian belief seven lives to finally enjoy an eternal relationship with him.

The encounter that night had changed me, my psyche and my total being. I now just belonged to the prince of my dreams. He was everything! My whole cosmos!

All the time I was waiting for him to turn up at my residence as he had divulged to Montgomery in the car on our way from Delhi to Solan.

I was waiting for his visit as a dying man waits for more life. I was waiting for him as in the old ballads, a lovelorn maiden, forsaken by her demon lover would wait in a romantic chasm, holy and enchanting.

But I was sure, one day, God would be gracious and there would be a consummation and a union between Vishal and me.

A few days later, I was informed that my father had expired. In fact he died a very pathetic death. He was coming home late and was all unsteady on the roadside. It was pouring and he could not see clearly. He fell down in the middle of the road. His head was crushed under a speeding truck that left no trace of it and sped away. There was no passer-by who could note the number of the truck. My father died then and there. Nobody came there to attend to the dead body. The dead body was crushed under truck after truck...it was a busy highway.

Montgomery by all standards was a great man. He never for a moment forgot what Vishal before, the real Vishal had said, "Always remember Montgomery that Durga is my wife, give her all the privileges due to my wife. She must get class I treatment."

Montgomery arranged a car for me and my brother to go to my village. I did not know why after all Montgomery was so exceptionally kind to me. I did not know that Vishal had himself confessed of his relationship with me.

When my car crossed the main street of Solan, incidentally, both the headmaster and the elected member were passing through the same road. It was the headmaster who first spotted me in the car.

He immediately pointed it out to his companion saying, "There's the bitch who not only slapped us hard but also blackened our faces."

"What do you want to do with her? We can today or tomorrow take our revenge on her right away. Let us throw acid on her face and burn her heavenly beauty to cinders. If she is not for us, she should not be left for anyone. I want to teach her a lesson never to come cross with males of the area, more particularly us."

The elected member said in a hushed voice, "Don't have anything to do with her. She is a modern woman. Educated, powerful and totally bestowed with the ideals of Swami Vivekananda and great Indian womanhood. That day God was gracious and she kind, therefore, we were left alive. Today if you come in her way, your generations will pay for it. Even the government of India is paying gallantry awards to women who show exemplary courage and bravery."

"You are a coward," the headmaster was irked.

But he was the first to clear the road, sooner than the elected member. He knew that if caught, his chances of escape would be no better than the chances of a toad under a road roller.

I was shocked at the death of my father. Daughters are no less great than sons. In matter of attachment to the parents, they are more attached to the parents than sons.

Though my father was a drunkard of the worst class, I was extremely pained. He was my father, and father and mother are the ones we fall back on.

I wanted him to be with the family if not to love us, at least to hate and hit us. But who could bring my father back to life?

The world is transitory. Those who have come have to go back. Nothing is immortal. Nothing remains.

Drinks and drugs have devoured thousands!

Stupid people who abort their daughters!

Sinners and damned hellish souls!

A world without girls will be devoid of love, grace, charm and all the finer sensibilities. The world will become unlovable. It will be no better than a burial ground.

Be it east or west. Daughters are the best!

The worst of the sights that I witnessed back home was of my mother. Malti was a great mother. But above all she was a great wife. After my invalid brother Jaggi and I came to my place of posting in the Mother India School, she could comfortably come and stay with me. But she held back on the pretext that she preferred the work of cleaning utensils and sweep other peoples' houses. I felt she was true about it but realised now that it was not so. In fact, she presented another form of feminine excellence.

Though she was abused everyday and frequently beaten black and blue, still she stayed back at Kalka because she wanted that her cruel drunkard husband should not sleep hungry. He must eat something.

She had overheard some elderly people say that if a drunkard ate a morsel after the drinks, he stood a better chance of living longer. She wanted her husband to live longer. If not for anything else, to be abused and beaten.

She had been so accustomed to her destiny and fate that she had no grudge with it. She took everything with stoic resignation. She wanted to live and die with her husband. Now when her husband had left her alone in the world, her only care and worry was my marriage. She had even selected a boy for me.

Next day early in the morning, she called me, "Durga my darling! You have seen the death of your father. Whatever he was is immaterial, he was my husband and your father, the like of whom there's none in the world.

"He has gone and I shall go too! I feel so lonely and helpless without him. However bad, a husband is a husband. I need to go to the other world to take care of him. May be even the fire of the bier has not been able to make him hate his drinks. He must be drinking there and I must go there to care for him."

I was aghast at the height of an Indian wife's fidelity. In my heart, I swore to be a wife like her. But a wife to whom?

The Chairman of the Group of Industries with whom, as an act of destiny, *I had had a marriage without marriage*!

'Although! He had forgotten everything in the operation, and now he talks to me as strangers do. He looks at me as if he has never seen me before, much less having made love to me.' I thought.

'Oh! His cringing for a kiss!
Oh! His slipping into my bed!

Oh! His catching my feet and shedding incessant tears for forgiveness and ending up in making love once again!
Oh! Those tears on my feet are my only witness. But wherefrom can I bring those tears back?
Oh! Cruel destiny! Why have you made a woman's heart so vulnerable?'

Once a woman falls for a man, she can never like any other. She can lie for anyone under the change of circumstances beyond her control!

But can she love the second and then third?

I had no idea! Or should I marry the man my mother was recommending and forget all about the Mother India School, the Chairman and the New York hospital.

Room number 11.

The room where I lost my virginity to a man whom I love, the Prince who had charmed me. I gave everything to him including my love and chastity and he had loved me more and more in return. We were married through our body and soul.

There was no dearth of handsome, attractive girls in this world. The Chairman was young and rich and the most eligible bachelor. Any family and any girl would fall for him. What would the stamp paper document concealed under my clothes do?

It was a confession of the Chairman's intimacy with me in private. A testimony to a *marriage without marriage*!

On a legal paper!

But what when now the Chairman does not recognise anything or anybody? Oh God! I shall commit suicide. Can Montgomery help? Should I go to him and beg for help?

No his daughters had to be married out of the Chairman's funds. That was the will.

Will which should have been implemented had the Chairman died. But he was alive.

Very much alive!

Sudha and her mother.

'I do not know what to do? I do need a friend to guide and help. To guide right and true!' I was puzzled.

I thought of my colleagues in the school. They were not dependable.

Yeh! My Haryanvi friend, Sneha. But her advice like her art was martial, she played Judo with all her problems.

Here was a very delicate matter and it must be discussed with somebody, empathetic, honest and God fearing.

'Who could it be better than my mother? She is a great woman. Though she is not educated but she is worldly wise.'

Weren't the world's greatest men, that Athenian, Socrates, totally illiterate?

Very often education is not help but bane of wisdom!

Weren't Chairman Sir and I, richly educated to commit that mistake? That horrible mistake!

That tragic error! That fatal flaw! I was totally romanticised and mesmerised when I thought of the room and the night, what happened there.

In my heart, I wanted it to happen again and again and again with him and him alone.

Oh, God! Make it happen! You can do it. God can do anything and everything. 'Ayurveda says, such patients come back some day, though, it does not say when?' This is what the doctor in New York had said. He was the chief of all the doctors. Yes!

I shall wait eternally. Forever. However I shall seek the advice of my mother in the evening. Yes this very evening!

In the evening, before I could open the case, my mother came to me and said, "Durga, I have seen a boy for you. He is of our caste. He belongs to a poor family like ours. I have known him from his childhood. The most wonderful thing about him is that he neither smokes nor drinks. He is tall and handsome. Please Durga, do not deny me. Do not give me any arguments else, I shall commit suicide. Till date you have not denied me a thing. This is the last thing I beg of you. Marry the boy and I shall leave for Haridwar. Otherwise, I shall commit suicide by taking poison or jumping into the river. Please, my good daughter. Say yes! And put alms into your mother's lap."

I did not know what to do? I was cut to the quick. I thought, 'I have lost my love. I have lost my father. I will lose my mother! I did not know where to go. I knew that my mother never gave empty threats. She meant every word she said. Even, when she said that she would go to the next world to be with my father.'

In order to put her off and not to break her heart, I said, "Mother, I shall talk to you about this at 8 p.m. I am too tired to talk of anything like this now."

Mother, in a way, took it as a sign of consent. Because, all able-bodied young women at the age of 22 or around would jump at the idea of their marriage for that is the age when a woman stands in full need of the match and is most willing though she herself would not admit openly. But all wise parents should know it.

She at once sent a message to Vinod and her family members to come to her house and see the girl as she was there for the day.

Vinod was certainly an eligible bachelor. He was Ph.D in English. At that time, he was working as an Inspector of Schools and was drawing a very handsome salary. His next promotion would be to the rank and position of D.E.O.

He came with his father, a retired S.H.O. of Kalka. In fact, Vinod and his family had heard a lot about my qualities of head and heart.

Above all my sterling beauty and strong character.

What passed between me and the Chairman in room number 11, nobody knew. It was known only to me, my Chairman, destiny and God.

My mother woke me up and wanted me to take a bath and look presentable. When I said, I would not, she cringed before me and said, "Durga, Please do it for my sake."

"But mother, it is winter and I took a bath in the morning fulsome."

"Please, Durga do it. Be a good daughter. There is a special reason. I shall tell you after you take bath."

When I was finished with my bath and all, my mother told me all about Vinod and their visit to our house at 8 p.m. They were punctual. Though we were poor, yet she had made some preparations to be served to the guests.

My first reaction was that I did not want to present myself to be seen by any other man. My hero and my ideal was Vishal, the Chairman.

But I had to submit before a torrent of tears from my mother. I said to her, "Okay mother! I agree to your request provided you will listen to my story afterwards and advise what I should do in the matter."

Mother thought for a while, there might have been some affair in the life of her daughter. Every girl in her youth has an affair or two. Simple. But marriage is a different matter. A lifelong affair!

Vinod looked at me and said, "There is no second opinion about the Taj. It is beautiful from all angles, in all seasons and weathers. From our side it is a yes! Total and complete! I shall keep her most carefully and lovingly."

The elders of the family wanted the boy and the girl to take a few minutes together to which I refused.

My mother took a minute to ask me separately if she should say yes.

I begged, "Mother, don't make any commitment. We will sit and discuss everything."

My mother accordingly, stated to the other party, "My daughter does not seem to be in a hurry. You will have to wait, a while. In fact her senior class students have to appear in their final exam. Their result in these finals will be counted in all their future tests and examinations and in more than a way decides Durga's Annual Report."

Vinod said approvingly, "We are in no hurry either. I still have to write four international papers after which I shall think of marriage. These papers will fetch me postings at major cities in India. They will also enable me to get better and quicker increments, every year. Of course, there should be an engagement sort of thing so that there is no uncertainty and each side is absolutely sure."

My mother was kind enough for me and said, "We will let you know," and the matter ended at that.

After they were gone, mother asked me, "Durga, I do not know why you did not agree to such an excellent proposal? Any other girl in your place would have jumped at such a wonderful offer. I expected a prompt answer from you, that too in the positive. Your indecisive approach has broken my heart and disheartened the callers. Before going, the boy's mother warned me, 'There are 5 other girls after us though our son likes Durga, the best of all.'"

I told my mother of the hardships that fell in my way and how everywhere goddess Durga saved me else by now I would have been reduced to cinders.

I held her hand and sat her next to me, "Mother dear! I shall tell you about the most secret part of my life unknown to anyone else in the world, except Vishal. He is the main character in this entire episode. He has lost his memory for a while but still I need you to listen to me. Nobody can take him or his memories from my heart and psyche. Mother! Please listen to every word that I speak, with utmost attention and care and then advise me accordingly. I need the advice of a sincere friend and there is no other sincere friend of a daughter than her own mother. Mothers have always been guiding the destiny of their daughters down the ages. Please don't leave me in lurch and guide me for the best. Please, mother dear."

It was around 3 a.m. when I finished the story of my life and sought my mother's advice in the matter.

After giving the matter a deep thought, my mother said, "Durga, you are first Vishal's. I would never ever ask you to desert the man, with whom you have had such a serious relation. Your encounter with him makes you more than a wife to him. You should have lived and died for him and I would not have bothered. But, the circumstances in your case are peculiar. One in a million!

"He cannot recognise you. He does not remember anything between the two of you. The unattested stamp paper has no validity in the eyes of law. Yours is a hopeless case. Besides, Vishal is very handsome, rich and propertied man. Many families and their daughters will be in queue to settle a matrimonial alliance with him. He will settle with any Indian beauty or a European blonde. The best is to forget about him. I am your mother. I cannot give you a wrong advice. The best is to forget about it all. Tear that stamp paper and put to an end, any record of the encounters between you two."

She virtually pulled that paper and tore it into a hundred pieces and let the torn papers fly into the storm blowing outside. Some bystanders said that they saw pieces of the paper flying towards the Chairman's residence too in the Solan district.

That was ostensibly the end of the love affair that could make me one of the most lovable wives who brought her husband back from the claws of death.

Next night, my mother shared with me how before meeting my father, she had once fallen in love with a military man, who had come on a vacation for two months. "Durga, for two months we loved each other as much as any man has ever loved a woman. I was virtually mad for him. Women really lose their poise when they fall in love for the first time. Then he was called back by the Forces because of the sudden hostility between India and Pakistan, if you remember in 1971 near Diwali, I was left heart broken. I thought somebody had snatched my life away from me. But I was helpless. I could do nothing but sulk in the corner of the house remembering Deepak. There was something else written for me. I had to live without him in the company of your father. Deepak was shot dead on the day of Diwali. It was a day of total darkness in my life. I married your father and forgot all about Deepak. Of course a cry comes out of my heart, sometimes, in the middle of night and mingles with the yells of the dead in a cremation ground.

"It was my luck that I got a drunkard husband, your father, though, there is no dearth of good men in this world." It was then that my mother thrust the photo of Vinod under my eyes.

Honestly speaking, I had no choice left for a bridegroom. Any man could be a good bridegroom. I had drunk in the nectar of Vishal's enormous love.

I had enjoyed a close proximity with my darling not once but for a whole night and the next day. Who could match those melodious harmonies that came out of his intimacy? Who could substitute those dancing celestial moments? A joy that had now taken flight! When shall return the glory of that time!

Oh! Never more! Oh! Never more!

My mother wanted a 'yes' right away. But I wanted some time. I also wanted to know Vinod more. Moreover, I was prepared to run away from the marriage altar, if Vishal showed some improvement.

I packed my luggage and left for the Mother India School, Solan. All the while I kept on praying to Lord, to set things right.

In the Bible, some sins have been detailed like lechery, gluttony, sloth, envy but, now I felt that the greatest is the sin of despondency.

It is a sin when we think that nothing can be done now.

It means that we negate the powers of the Almighty.

✦ ✦ ✦

VI

Okay Miss

We forget the fact that for God nothing is impossible.

He can do anything any time.

He can sprout springs of hopefulness out of hopelessness.

He can create life out of the dead.

He can make springs in the deserts.

I was always waiting for him to come to my residence. He had himself said, "I will pay a visit to her residence." Yes. This was what the Chairman had said. He gave me hope and I waited, waited, waited. I was waiting even today. I would wait endlessly.

Yes! God is really very gracious. Just after a week of my coming back with my mother after the funeral ceremony of my father at Kalka he really turned up.

It was yesterday only. Yes! Yesterday at 6 p.m.

Montgomery was with him. Without standing on any formality, he came out, "What was your name pretty Miss?" he asked.

"I am extremely sorry; I forgot your name," he quickly added.

I was cut to the quick when I learnt that not to speak of other things, he had forgotten my name also.

He said, "I have come to take a cup of tea at your place. But you know there was another purpose added as well. I have heard a lot about your capabilities as a teacher as also an expert at life. You are a connoisseur. While the two of us take tea, Montgomery will show you some ten photographs of young pretty girls.

"They all want to marry me, some for my property and some for my youth. I want a girl who has a heart of gold, who is feminine and courageous, all the same."

He added further, "I have heard you have a great insight to human psyche. Please find out the best girl for me. I want to get married within three months and handover some of my responsibilities to a befitting wife."

I saw that Montgomery had noticed the stream of tears that trickled down my eyes, though I tried hard to hide the torrent of tears.

Even the Chairman felt something unusual. Therefore, he said, "I quite understand that a decision of this magnitude requires time and peace...a decision on which my entire future life depends! Montgomery, I shall not be able to come to her residence because of work pressure. However, you must know that your Chairman is a man of his word. I shall go by her decision."

He added, "I do not know, in her I see somebody who belonged to me in some life, really. For three days, she must be left on her own and on the fourth day, collect from her the picture she most likes. Give that picture to me and discard the rest. I shall do what she wishes me to do."

I saw tears in the eyes of the manager.

The Chairman's final words were, "Okay Miss! See you after this, probably at yours or my marriage, whichever is earlier."

He added, "The dress you wear on either of the occasions will be a gift from me for making my selection."

He turned to Mr. Montgomery and said, "Buy her the best dress that is available. Don't mind the money. These are my orders and if you fail to comply, you will be fired."

The Chairman left, followed by the manager.

All the time he spent at my place, my mother stole many looks of the Chairman, from all angles I guess.

When the Chairman left in his attractive and shimmering new Mercedes, my mother just rushed to me and embraced me. She said, "What a handsome man Durga! He is Adonis. Even the best of the virgin will fall for him.

"And the circumstances you narrated, in which he wanted to be taken to heaven with the touch of a pretty damsel like you, none could withstand his overwhelming personality."

She further said, "In his totality, he is a man, any woman would like to seduce and if not agreeing, then plead with him, but make him one with her to be canonised forever." Listening to what my mother said, I burst out into the loudest of the cries that made the demons in the trees gather in a conference to check if another soul, lost to human kind could be mixed with the realm of their chief, Satan.

Having emptied my distress through my eyes, I said, "It is a strange world where nothing is in the hands of man. Great

Greek playwrights, Sophocles, Achilles, Euripides in the hoary past tried to sort of this question. Is destiny character or Is character destiny? Homer, Virgil, Dante, Shakespeare, Kalidas, and great religious prophets and saints, all addressed to this fundamental question."

I added, "All have given their different interpretations of the real crux of life. But this basic question defying all interpretations continues, unabated, unanswered.

"Had God wanted it, today I would have been the queen of this kingdom. Now I stand here selecting a bride for a man who was my bridegroom for that one night! I stand here to find my rival, and to give over with my own hands what I so madly want for myself."

Tears started flowing incessantly from my eyes and I wondered at my fate. What a fool it had made of me.

My mother was also weeping, hiding herself in the bathroom thinking of what had passed in the life of her daughter. Earlier, she had thought, that there was something wrong with me to ignore or take light of such an eligible bachelor. Vinod was young. He was handsome. He was drawing a good salary. He was Ph.D in English. But could he stand a comparison to the dignified, graceful, monarchical man, the Chairman?

Oh! No. Oh! Never!

I was true to my duty. My great teacher of school, Ragini from whom I learnt so many things in life, told me, "Always keep duty above everything else."

She had said, "Duty is divine! It must be kept above self. It must not be allowed to mix with any other consideration."

I therefore kept on weighing all the different photos to spot the perfect woman who could best suit my beloved.

Finally, my choice fell on the girl with black jeans and a yellow top. However, to make the perfect choice and avoiding a blame, should the proposal fail, I sent a message to the manager. I discussed openly with him, "Manager Sir, you can tell the Chairman, that I have selected the girl for him and according to me, she suits the Chairman perfectly well. However, I wanted that he should meet with the girl and then finalise the whole thing."

As I was talking, he was looking into my eyes, watching the quantum of pain behind my words. Somehow I had resigned myself to fate, to the hard divine will.

I said to myself, 'Durga! Only the divine will operate. Nothing else counts!'

I was further surprised by this Chairman's strength of character. Though he appreciated my beauty but the idea of using me never occurred to him.

In beauty and grace, I was one in a million.

I was bewitchingly charming.

Charmingly bewitching.

I was certainly the most beautiful of the 10 girls in the pictures put together.

He could come to my room. He knew that I was staying alone with my mother. He could love me and I wanted to be loved. Anytime any day! Though I couldn't confess before others. But I wanted my Vishal to call me, 'Dorris, darling!' In spite of my principles and resolutions, after the encounters in room number 11 at New York I wanted him so madly. But what a character of a man!

Unheard of!

Unthought of!

Not to speak of meeting me secretly, he had not even tried to look at me.

Something unusual in the world where men would follow ladies like hounds.

I wished to make my last try. To try the last arrow from my feminine quiver. Since, it was his work; he would very much like to come over.

Besides, when a man gets to meet a woman in private, open to speak his heart and do a little romancing, how could he deny?

My idea of the male sex was formed by the headmaster, the elected member and above all the four hounds I came across in the paddy fields.

I had no one else other than my brother, and being differently able I felt he was bereft of any sexual feelings.

I had asked the manager to ask the worthy Chairman to make it convenient to come in the evening. My purpose was to see and welcome him alone. If he did not bring the prospective bride, I would be only too glad, I thought. May be a repetition of the act of room number 11 would bring back lost memories.

Therefore, I cooked an early meal and requested my mother, "Please mother. Take the meal early and sleep in brother's room, I have some very important answer sheets to check. There may also come some people to meet me."

My mother, being an experienced old lady, understood everything. She knew I was still trying to get back my love!

She said with utter seriousness, "Durga, I am also tired. I cannot stay awake tonight. I shall go to bed early."

Hardly as she left for her room, I came into the washroom, looked at myself into the mirror. Though as usual, I was as beautiful and graceful I always was I wanted to enhance my charm still more.

I switched on the geyser. To my ill luck, it was not working properly. No chance. I touched the cold water of the tank. It was freezing. Still I decided to take a bath.

To my utter dismay, the Chairman's message had come through the manager, "I am sending the bride to be, in the company of the manager. She will stay with you as long as you want, even the whole night. Have a friendly chat and when you have made the decision, call the manager, he will drop her home." All parties were dissatisfied.

I was pained beyond measure, for understandable reasons.

The future bride too wanted some time with the husband to be. Montgomery could not do anything even though he was all out for me.

Before leaving, he had a few more words from the Chairman, "Madam please see that the girl is good in looks and virtues. Above all he wants a girl with resistance."

And the manager, added, "May be within him, he is still searching you, Durga!"

Montgomery said and left. I asked him to come after an hour.

I thought to myself, 'What am I to do with the girl throughout the night? Only if in her place was Vishal himself!'

I was transported to the days in the big city.

New York!

Passing an hour with the prospective bride was a punishment of the worst kind as I was not at all interested in the girl.

I was interested in my darling! But I was surprised to his unusual resistance, his unflinching mind.

When Mr. Montgomery returned after an hour, I told him, "Tell the worthy Chairman my vote is for Reena," for that was her name. How would I tell you how happy the girl was feeling!

She thought, I had made her a millionaire and the wife of one of the richest business magnets of the state.

"Oh! Blind to fate. Had it been within my powers, I would never have allowed my sweetheart to be snatched away even by Diana or Venus herself."

I learnt after a week that Chairman had made it public that he was getting married to Reena, after three months on 11th of February.

Now, it was my mother's turn to pay a visit to Vinod's house and announce my acceptance of the proposal. She also had to ask about further proceedings in the matrimonial matter.

Vinod who was a gentleman to the core spoke most politely to my mother, "Mother! My final paper is to be written in January. Thereafter, we can get married. Other details are to be finalised by the elders and I have nothing to do about that." My mother suggested, "I can give you Durga's cell number in case you would like to call her sometime."

He quickly replied, "In such matters I think nothing before the actual marriage. Once the marriage is performed, the husband and wife have hundreds of hours to talk to each other, whatever they want to do, nothing before that."

Meanwhile his mother came and said with the authority enjoyed by the mother of the bridegroom in India, "Sister, I have consulted the priests and according to the horoscopes the only suitable date for marriage is 5th of February. Please see that there cannot be a change in what the stars say. We attach a lot of faith on the celestial bodies, the stars." After some other preliminaries, my mother came home and told me that 5th of February had been fixed for my marriage.

When I was told about the date, I was not happy. Somehow, I wanted to get married after the Chairman for reasons not logical or scientific in any way. So as far as the question of money was concerned, Vinod's family had made it clear that they wanted to keep it a rather simple affair.

But Vinod wanted to make it a big show. He was doubly happy. He had got the promotion to the rank of D.E.O. and had become the educational head of the district and it was a highly authoritative post. He would sit and talk with DC, SMO, SSP and other high rank officers. He had also been given a very good accommodation in the officer's colony.

Something else was also brewing up alongside. There were three persons who did not want this marriage to be a success. In fact if possible, they wanted to crack, this marriage even before it really took place.

They were Sudha, headmaster and the elected member. All the three had different reasons to bring chaos and devastation upon the two persons yet to be married because of different reasons.

Sudha, in fact was in her teens, and yet a school going girl, when she first spread her lustful tentacles towards Vinod who was then pursing an M.A. Sudha would come to Vinod's house, since she was besotted by his looks.

She would then try all her tricks but failed each time. Finally, one day, she found Vinod alone, studying in a separate room. No one was expected for about two hours. She thought she would succeed in seducing him that day. She was dressed up accordingly.

Vinod's refusal made Sudha revengeful. She had avowed herself to teach him a lesson of his life.

While Sudha was trying to entrap him into kissing her, he pushed her back, throwing her mercilessly on the floor and leaving immediately. He believed that since Sudha belonged to his city, she was a sister and never could be a beloved. But Sudha had not forgiven him for not yielding and showing disrespect to a girl grown up enough to fall in love.

Moreover, though, I never harmed her even in my wildest imagination, she harboured a grudge against me and held me responsible for her failure with her one time most targeted lover, Vinod.

The headmaster was afraid that if I talked to Vinod about how he tried to rape me in the hotel, he would find a hundred and one ways to throw him out of the job. He being the DEO was in the capacity and position to hit him hard leading to his termination from the service.

He did not want termination under any circumstances. All his children had yet to be settled. His daughters were yet to be married and he had to attend to a number of family obligations. He had an old mother. Her eyes needed to be operated at a good hospital. Money was needed for all these things. Out of his job, his salary would stop and it would become difficult to defray all these expenses.

The elected member knew that Vinod was a big shot, and he had direct contacts with the MP and the MLA. He wanted to contest the ensuing election to become the President of the Committee, to begin with and then to proceed further be the MLA.

He thought that all his evil deeds had still been out of the knowledge of the people. Compared with the other candidates he stood better chances because he was a Brahmin and most of the people of the area were Brahmins. He was an expert at exploiting the sentiments of the locals. He could give a quick and convincing colour to caste politics.

Neither of the two exhibited any sense of compassion or sensibilities although they belonged to the upper castes and learned communities.

They were waiting for a good opportunity. I attended the ring ceremony of the Chairman on purpose. I wanted to see what the ring given to the bride looked like.

Yes, it was the same ring, the same costly ring, perhaps running into millions of rupees which the Chairman had once presented to me in those moments of utter passion in the New York hospital, room number 11.

It was studded with diamonds.

I could not, despite my whole might, stop the torrent of tears from my eyes and went to the wash room to wipe my face with gallons of water. I relived the whole scene of room number 11 in the Washington hospital. Some memories get so deeply embedded in our psyche and pierce through our soul in an inseparable way. Water could wash my tears, but not my pain and grief.

My heart was bleeding silently and profusely. After some time, I rejoined the ceremonies.

To my surprise, the Chairman came over by my side and said, "Madam! I have gone by your choice in the selection. I do not know why there is a part of my heart that always wants to care for you and you alone in the entire world? I think you and I have had some kind of association in the past lives.

"The moment I see you, a kind of orchestra begins to play in my heart. I am at once carried to some distant mountains and hills and vales and dales. It appears that there must have been a connection between you and me in some passionate way. The moment I look at you the palpitation of my heart increases and I feel irresistibly drawn towards you. Can you tell me why?"

I had no words to answer him, just a blank stare. As though searching for an answer himself, he said, "I am sure there certainly is some reason, known to the gods may be, and hidden from us. I don't know whether it is right or wrong... but...but I need to confess this to rid myself of any guilt before I start my new life. Sometimes I am shaken up in the middle of the night. I feel as if I have wronged you in some way and that my conscious would not let me forget it.

"I feel as though there is a part of me left with you...you are my employee, I know I cannot have a relation with you but only if you could explain why am I not able to let go of your thoughts?"

I cannot explain in words, the thrill I experienced. Every pore of my body was overjoyed at the expression of his love. I was intoxicated. I could not control myself. I wanted to remind him of the beautiful bond of love that had so strongly connected us on the night of 22nd.

Just then the bride's mother called for him. The Chairman had to leave.

I wanted to hold him, and tell him, 'You are still my Lord! I am untouched by any other man.'

I wondered, 'One thing was sure, there was something in the Chairman's consciousness seated deep down, forcing to be born.'

'Is he likely to remember the past?' I muttered to myself.

That night I could not sleep and decided and undecided and resolved and unresolved a hundred times. I remember the doctor say, "Some of these cases came back to normalcy." Only if God brought him back to me and bless me. Life without him was drab. True heaven existed in his eyes! In his hug were hidden the treasures of the nine worlds. I had tasted the honey in his sweet talk, ambrosia in his love and heaven in his company. Oh! God help me meet my mate!!!

Finally, I came to the conclusion that his remembering the past was just a figment of my imagination. Leaves that fall off the branches never go back up again. The dead do not rise from the graves. Time once gone cannot be recalled. An unhinged brain cannot come back to normalcy.

Moreover, any kind of nearness with the Chairman would destroy Reena's matrimony and married life. I did not want to do that under any circumstances.

After making up my mind to keep away from all thoughts of the Chairman I slept for the remaining 2 hours of the night. When I got up I felt heaviness in my head. I did not know why walking, talking, sleeping or awake, I could not forget him though I would always resolve not to let his thoughts bother me. The more determined I was to avoid him, the more forcefully he thrust on to my consciousness.

I thought, 'My mother has suffered her whole life. I am her only support. At Kalka, she used to clean people's utensils, sweep their houses, and wash their dirty linen...a real tough job because it is done without any sense of involvement; it becomes a torture, a taxing work of useless drudgery. When a woman performs these chores for her own house...it is different. I had made her leave her source of income. She was my responsibility.

'I was young and energetic. I wanted to give her some days and weeks of rest, calm and carefree life. I wanted to ensure that she lived the remaining part of her life not as somebody's servant-maid but as my mother. I had decided that I would cook and she would eat. I would wash her clothes along with mine and clean her utensils. She is my mother and not a slave!

'I shall show her all good things of life. I shall never discuss my sorrows before her or with her. I shall do my utmost to keep her happy and content.

'Jaggi, my brother, could neither walk nor sit properly. After the thrashing he received by those two villains, he became worse. He loved me very dearly. He was my brother. The only one brother. He was beaten and thrashed and pushed into the drain because he was my brother!

'I shall punish the guilty for torturing an invalid, for manhandling a cripple. If other people had not intervened on grounds of mercy, they would have killed him. See the audacity of the bastards, they could attempt to kill somebody who could not sit properly or walk. God damn them!

'I shall have to live for their sake. I am not interested in the marriage. But I will have to marry for them. At present it is not I but they who are more important. I am confident about my beauty and I know I shall remain so for at least 15 more years. My life will always be in danger from lustful men. I know I can brave it all and may break their bones with my Judo, but then the hurt dogs will catch hold of my brother or my old mother and take their revenge on them.

'I shall have to marry Vinod, though my heart and soul will forever belong to Vishal. Marriage is my necessity. Neither for sex nor for pleasure!

'I will always believe that those encounters in the hospital room were worth a thousand times and had rested my sexual desires forever. Now I want a husband for namesake. A paper tiger husband to let the ruffians know, not to look at me with lustful eyes as I now belonged to someone else, I was also the one who had a husband. It was my destiny. It was written on the lines on my palm.

'It seemed His will and so must take place.

'Yes! I shall bow to it and say most willingly.'

Let thy will be done.

The time for marriage always seems distant but it never is. It soon passes and then comes the momentous day. My ring ceremony took place. Vinod had called a large number of his friends, partly to share the festivities and chiefly to show how exceptionally beautiful his bride was.

It was now that Vinod talked to me, in more of a formal tone than in the intimate one that such an occasion demanded.

He just asked me, "How do you feel? Are you happy? Will you serve my parents after marriage or just ignore them?"

I did not answer any of his questions. I just smiled and that was all.

The day of marriage was drawing near. Neither I, nor Vinod talked or initiated any dialogue. I was too engrossed in the thoughts of my lost love. Thinking about him being peaceful enough.

Vinod was a scholar in the real sense and was always thinking of either writing a new paper for the international journals or improving an old one.

My heart lay in Vishal's bosom. Vinod's heart lay in books.

Moreover, Vinod was an old-fangled man and believed that for love to be honest and true, it must originate after marriage. I too was like this once. But in my case, a sudden incident in room number 11 at New York changed me and my Indian philosophy forever. I came to realise that love was a great force and was beyond being circumscribed by any geographical or national boundaries or philosophies.

My mother was like the old ladies taking a lot of interest in all things. She once met Vinod by chance, and asked him slyly, "You can come to meet her in our house if you so like, sometimes. Now times have changed, and I am a modern woman."

She just braced her personality in her new dress to assert that she really was a modern lady and not an old hag.

"All connections after marriage." Vinod said and let the matters rest there.

The Chairman did not come to attend my ring ceremony. I thought that he had done it on purpose or may be Reena had asked him not to have anything to do with my ring ceremony. I was sure he would not come on my marriage either.

But, come what may, I was bent upon wearing his suit, the special suit, brought by Montgomery on the night of my marriage.

Back home in India Sudha was once again in the arms of her first lover who was a die-hard alcoholic. He did not do anything worthwhile and was a swindler, a cheat, a thief and a womaniser, all in one. Still, he was lucky. He was born under a gracious star. Despite being unemployed and frustrated, he would always succeed in making some money by hook and crook. He also had sexual relations with some lewd women to satisfy his lust.

Now Sudha had come.

He told Sudha what woman of her kind generally liked to listen, "You are my only love! Your absence from the city killed me completely. I was always thinking of you, day in and day out. It was very difficult to pass time. Thrice I thought of committing suicide. But your love saved me. Once I lay on the railway line after drinking rather too heavily. That day the train had already left and there was only one train at 8 p.m. daily. I had a very sound sleep on the railway track. Next day I found the village stray dog licking my face right there where you kiss me so madly."

He further added rather seductively, "Second time again, God saved me for your love. You are such a sweet darling. This time, I thought of committing suicide by hanging myself with a rope. Yes! I had already spotted the place where I would hang myself. Now only a rope was needed from the bazaar. I planned first to buy the rope and then to drink. Oh! Drinking is a must for a drunkard like me."

Adding to the climax, he continued, "Then I thought that I must first drink and then bring the rope. In a drunken state, I would be more determined and could buy a rope of the proper strength and length. You know, I am a rather heavy man.

"After consuming a bottle and a half I was about to reach the shop to buy the rope. With my distorted condition I could not see the approaching elephant, only hear the cries of the children shouting elephant, elephant. It however appeared no bigger than a bull after the drinks to me. I thought I should make the purchase and rush off. The auspicious time of hanging was passing. I was too heavily drunk to make the right purchase.

"I could not tell the shop keeper what I really wanted to buy and why, so I asked him to give me something to bind. He was very busy at that time because a pretty female customer had come in the shop for the first time in a week. He thought, I wanted a string for my trousers and gave me so. Intoxicated that I was I thought it to be the rope and reached back with the most unsteady steps.

"Somehow I put the string around my neck. Because of the kick of the drink, I fell on the floor. I thought, I had been hanged and the last couple of breaths were left. People utter religious incantation to save themselves from the perils of hell. I started uttering your name repeatedly with all religiousness."

By this time, Sudha was also intoxicated, under the influence of his love talk and liquor. She had started taking liquor in the company of her English husband, Spenser.

She also took drugs, with Sunny Sharma.

Sunny asked her, "Sudha did you fall in love with anybody in America?"

Sudha replied, "Oh! Not at all. I am as I left you, for you and you alone."

She switched off the light and started making love to her lover.

Spenser the ward boy at the hospital and her husband from the US had packed up for India to know about his wife, Sudha. Spenser may have been a labourer, but he had a big heart and a soul to support it.

✦ ✦ ✦

VII

Double Standard of Morality

When he came to New York, from Washington, he had left his dog behind with a neighbour.

Twice he flew to Washington from New York only when he learnt that his dog was sick. He went there patted his dog, got medicines for it and flew back.

There was no dearth of women, even wives in America.

He was rich to afford half a dozen women. But in Sudha's case, firstly he had married her properly and secondly; he was worried that she may be in some difficulty. If she was okay in India, going well with any Tom, Dick or Harry, it was a different issue. In that case there was no burden on his soul.

He flew to India to see the things for himself and decide once and for all with Sudha, this way or that, without feeling bad in either case for that was their culture in America. If Sudha wanted to come back to America, he would welcome her irrespective of the encounters she would have had in India.

He himself had many encounters with a couple of blondes. How could he blame Sudha?

Thomas Hardy in his famous novels Tess, Jude the Obscure and Mayor of CasterBridge had vehemently attacked the double standard of morality in matters of sex and argued that in these matters also, as in others, men and women were equal. Initially, Hardy's books were burnt at the Broadway Square, London. But subsequently his philosophy was adopted as a way of life in the entire Western and North American countries.

It is now being put more and more in practice in modern India also. If you want your wife to be a Sita, you have to become a Rama.

Great! Every sensible and reasonable man must accept it.

Spenser reached Solan outside Sudha's house, on the same winter night. She was with Sunny Sharma, her fiancé, in the dark room.

Spenser being ignorant of the approach to an Indian house just banged against their door. Not expecting anybody at that time, the carefree lovers had not bolted the door. The door flung open. And in the moonlight, Spenser saw his wife with somebody else. The view was rather clear because of the full moon night.

Spenser at once said, "I am sorry, very sorry to disturb! Please continue!" and he hurried out.

Spenser conducted himself very well. He did not stay back to talk to anybody. All his questions had been answered.

He just praised in his heart, the words of William Shakespeare, 'Frailty thy name is woman.'

He caught the first flight back and reached his own country with a different set of moralities now.

Sudha wanted to face the situation boldly and speak clearly.

She had decided to tell Spenser straightway, "I have no ill will against you. You were a fairly good man. But the barrier of language between us was the only hurdle." Luckily, Spenser left without meeting her and there was no need for clarifications.

Sunny Sharma there on, many times mentioned to Sudha about how he needed to be taken to the doctor as he had hallucinations at night. For the recent instance, he would say that he saw a white man in his room staring at him most intently...that was actually not there, probably.

Sudha did not tell him anything about her American husband Spenser or his visit to their room when they were together in a compromising position. Why should she tell that she married someone in America if she could hide?

Sudha's mother had gone into depression when her daughter had failed to marry Vishal. She was now languishing in a civil hospital for a while. Sudha was happy with Sunny Sharma. Sudha was however very bitter with me. She still wanted to take revenge on me if only she could get an opportunity.

Sudha did not want to let me succeed with Vishal. When she failed to get him, and when Reena was engaged to him through a formal ring ceremony, Sudha heaved a sigh of relief. Inwardly, as we know she had so much wanted to marry Vinod also.

But he had insulted her away. Ignored her and even spat on her face. She was a woman who never gave up. She wanted a day when Vinod would come to her, beg from her amorous pleasures, and she would show him the way.

She would spit at him and show him that a woman always remained superior to a man in such circumstances.

Though it was perhaps not that easy but you never know. But once Vinod married a celebrated beauty like Durga such chances would just vapourise as Vinod may not see this way or that. And her vengeance would never be satisfied!

Sudha was a kind of woman who could take any decision. Who could do anything to satisfy the vengeance of her heart. One who could commit the deadliest of deeds to attain her ugly and wicked design.

Jealousy and envy in women reign ever supreme.

Of late, she had started going to a man who used to deal with the supernatural. Sudha's mother wanted the help of this supernatural man for the fulfilment of the desires of her daughter. She also felt that I was the cause of her daughter going astray. She after appeasing the ghostly man got from him a kind of poison using which, a person would go mentally sick and diseased. This poison was to be mixed in tea or milk or any liquid.

Sudha wanted to administer it to me on the night of my marriage and silently madden me out of wits. I did not know it.

The only thing that weighed heavily on my heart was why the Chairman did not come to attend my ring ceremony? Was it possible that he may not come to attend the marriage as well? It was only his will whether he would come or not. I had no control on the Chairman, anyways. He was the master and I, a mere employee.

In fact the Chairman and the manager had gone to New York for a business trip. I had no idea about it. Since, the manager was a very intelligent man, the Chairman had developed a deep trust in him. He would take him into confidence in many matters.

At New York, while there was some time left for their flight for India, an idea flashed in the mind of the manager that he should get the Chairman examined in the hospital. He was a great man who loved the Chairman from the core of his heart and also wanted to help me.

But what if the hospital staff asked for the Chairman's pretty wife? The Chairman would certainly like to know who was referred to as his pretty wife. Then would arise the question whether he was a married or not?

The manager thought these questions were hard to be answered. Instead of making things clear, the visit would make matters worse. Thus, the two of them, did not go anywhere and caught the flight back to India and reached Solan.

When I learnt that the Chairman did not come to attend to my ring ceremony because he was away to New York, I was at peace. New York reminded me of a number of other things also which were now of no use except to look back in spare time and be pained.

By now I had become stoic. I knew that it was destiny that decided things. There was nothing one could do.

I was reminded of the two lines of the famous Persian poet Omar Khayyam, translated into English by Fitzgerald:

> *'The moving finger writes and having written moves on,*
> *Neither all thy piety nor wit, shall remove a line or word please bring it below Neither!'*

Next week was my marriage. It was arranged as per the dictates of my would be mother-in-law. Indian womanhood is a picture of sacrifice and self denial.

I wanted to commit suicide but I was living for my brother Jaggi and my suffering mother. My life and charm practically had ended with the Chairman's operation not going right in New York hospital.

Indian marriage is an elaborate program extending into many days. So many formalities needed to be done. Though it is a mingling of the two bodies at the end, yet it must be properly preceded with a number of formalities. Without these, marriage is not complete and is not said to be properly solemnised.

This is what I had stressed when the Chairman wanted me in room number 11 of the hospital. The Chairman was mad to own me. Every atom of his body was seething to mingle with mine, harmoniously and rhythmically, but I like a stupid cat was showing unnecessary resistance.

I thought, 'Any other girl at my place mustn't have shown that stupid resistance. I should have made a movie of the whole thing with his consent. I should have put on that diamond ring which now Reena is wearing, coming into the Chairman's family from generations.

'If I had been practical and pragmatist, I should have contacted the staff on duty of the hospital. Told our mutual desire to be one in the hospital room, and done the same thing which all married couples do, married with or without the rituals.'

I mused further, 'Yes, I was foolish to act that night. I should have taken the legal papers signed by the attorney. Today nobody could challenge those solid documents Vishal had got made for me and was presenting me before anything. But I became too fussy. So I must repent for those stupidities. I viewed with lusterless eyes and unenthusiastic fervour, those very formalities being performed in my house now and the more I looked at those formalities and rituals the more I cursed myself.'

I thought, 'One single mistake can change the course of the coming fifty years. That single mistake will now not make me the mother of the Chairman's children, do what I may. This nagging mother-in-law would not have become the grandmother of my children!'

This is what might have been. Like Charles Lamb's essay, Dream children: things could have been different if God had wanted it to be that way. And had I acted a little wisely. But destiny!

Thomas Hardy's Immanent Will, Sophocles' Nemesis.

William Shakespeare's famous lines:

'As flies to wanton boys are we to the gods.

They kill us for their sport.'

Christopher Paolini's: What will be will be.

Indian philosophy as contained in the Geeta where Lord Krishna ordained, Do thy action, reward is not thy concern.'

Suddenly, an inner awakening dawned upon me. I felt some kind of nobility. I had not acted in a mean way. I conducted myself as any Indian girl would. The rituals and formalities were not made overnight. These contain the wisdom of ages.

At least I had the satisfaction that I obeyed my conscience.

I said to myself, 'Given the similar circumstances, I shall act the same way again. Not one time but again and again till I mix with dust.'

I cried, 'Oh God! Give me the courage to stand on my own. Save my soul as you saved your son, Christ. I am also your daughter! Though a fallen one!'

As if it was some divine intervention, I heard some voice, "Do not lament of your action. Who says you did a particular action? Who are you to do any action? You never are the doer. You never do things, things are done unto you."

I had a hallucination. I saw, Lord Krishna with his flute saying, "It is I not you. Bow to the divine will. Only say, Let thy will be done."

I was suddenly discharged of the useless agitations and tribulations. I thought if I would have broken the law of Diana of my own accord and my Chairman had subsequently refused to marry me in the earnest. What then? Anything could happen. Therefore blow with the wind and flow with the tide.

I looked at the formalities of that day; those had been over while I was busy with the thoughts of my past. Those formalities and rituals I, at once, thought to be very important, that minutes ago seemed to be all useless and irrelevant.

Now three days had been left for my marriage and less than a week's time was left for Vishal's. All this while, Vishal had not made any effort to talk to me. He was totally silent. I do not know why I did not have any means of knowing the facts. I believed only in one thing as I said confided in Sneha.

Blow with the wind and flow with tide.

Sneha had been happily married by now and was helping us out along with her husband Harish. Even the news of the outside world would come to me through this couple.

By the outside world I meant, a world in which Vishal and I did not exist, others did. In my world there was only one man, not Vinod but Vishal and I believed that it would continue to be so unless the holy fire of the altar burnt the feelings of Vishal from my mind and made way for Vinod.

I thought, 'I am not the only girl who has had a relationship before marriage. As a matter of fact there is hardly one who has not had. All fade away with the passage of time. It is not a must that all such relationships must end in matrimonial alliance. Further, very often these relationships turn out to be utter failures.'

I was reminded; an ancient Indian sage prophesied in the most pithy and pregnant words a great truth, 'Where there is love without marriage, there must be marriage without love.'

I thought my love had failed, may be my marriage would also fail.

Next day, Sneha whose husband too was in the teaching profession, a headmaster, brought rather startling news. She said, "Durga, do you remember those two bastards the headmaster and the elected member who attempted an unsuccessful rape on you, way back?"

"Yes I do. What of those?"

"They are mortally afraid of you. The headmaster worried that his job is in danger as your husband, Vinod is a big shot. He can chuck him out of the job if only you complained against him. Your husband enjoys a reputation of being a relentless officer who does not forgive such persons and gives them exemplary punishment so that it must be a strong deterrent for the others." Sneha added, "He has talked about all this to my husband and wants to use my friendship with you, to request you to forgive him and he assures he will never ever repeat such a blunder. So is the elected member, he is afraid that your would be husband's nearness to DC and the SSP may not only spoil his chances of a ticket in the elections but also put him behind the bars."

I at once sent the message to the two of them that past was past and I had now no ill will against them and that they should not be afraid at all. The message was duly delivered through Harish.

But wicked people are tortured from inside and never can leave their vicious nature. Both of them were planning to take no chances. They wanted to pull out the evil from the roots. They planned something blessed by Satanic forces but watched over by the divine. At the same time, Sudha was keeping that deadly poison that maddened a person completely to be administered to me in the milk given to me.

Time runs in different cases at different speed.

My day of marriage had come and there was a lot of hustle and bustle. Entire staff members of the Mother India School, both teaching and non teaching had come together in three buses. Some senior students too had requested the administration for they wanted to join the marriage ceremony of the most popular and meritorious teacher of the school.

The class 4 union of the school did not want to be left behind and had approached the manager to be taken to the ceremony in the school bus.

Nobody knows, not even the Chairman himself, why he called the manager with an urgent order and said, "Montgomery, spend as much money as needed on Durga's marriage and make it a memorable occasion. I shall also join the party."

On the other side, the elected member was conspiring with the headmaster, "Do what you can? How you can? When you can? Destroy the two of them. About 6 persons are at your beck and call. I want total and complete result."

The priest was the first to come to recite the mantras.

The poison vial was concealed inside Sudha's purse. The milk for me was prepared and Sudha emptied her bottle of poison.

All went to bring the bride.

The maid of the house Syba along with Jaggi saw Sudha's mother come hurriedly and take the poisoned milk kept for me to the last drop and left for wilderness from wither. She had come there, brought by divinity to punish the wicked. She was too hungry to resist the glass of milk.

The maid rushed in and brought a fresh glass of milk in place of the old one. She was afraid that if the auspicious glass was not found full of milk when the bride came to take it, her own job may go. She would be fired.

In the dress bought by the Chairman's ambassador, Montgomery, I looked ravishing, as if a real fairy descended from the heaven.

I took the auspicious milk presented to me by Sudha, unsuspicious of what a woman could do to a woman.

Sudha was unaware that the wheel had come a full circle and she, with the intention to poison me had poisoned her own mother. She left fearing that she may be caught.

As I tiptoed towards the altar, the Chairman along with Montgomery walked into the pandal. The four eyes met and wanted them to be reminded of all that had happened in room number 11 in New York. But alas! Nothing like that happened! Now the last moment in the marriage of the girl came when according to the Indian tradition the seven rounds are taken by the bride and the bridegroom around the holy fire after which the bride belongs to the bridegroom for all intents and purposes and they can do anything, go anywhere and enjoy their youthful life ahead.

Montgomery, the pious soul made a fervent appeal to the merciful heavens, "Oh! God! The last minute has come. I have been worshipping you, believing in you for more than half a century and I have never ever asked you for anything in return, please save this girl. She is innocent and pious. Ah Christ's Blood! Oh Virgin Mary! If you do not protect her, I shall never speak anything in praise of the Lord."

Hardly the second round had gone by and I saw fire everywhere. There was devastating fire all around. Jaggi, and the house watchman Sham Bahadur had seen the headmaster and the elected member light the fire with the help of half a dozen accomplices.

Next moment, a heavy burning sleeper from the top fell down and struck the Chairman's head. He fell down with a thud. But the next moment, as if pulled up by the god of Love, Cupid himself, he stood up like a military commander and shouted, "Dorris! Durga!!! Dorris!!!"

On the stage as I shrieked looking at Vishal, he rushed towards me shouting and bleeding profusely, "Dorris! What's going on? You are mine and mine you shall remain."

I at once opened the matrimonial knot from the trousseau with Vinod and within a minute we were in each other's tight embrace, eyes closed in full view of thousands of people who were rushing for their lives. They had never seen a spectacle like this. They did not know if they had come to the marriage of Vinod the teacher, or the great Chairman.

I saw that Montgomery the efficient man at once take charge of the situation. He gave us his hurried blessings, thanked the angels and called the ambulance and other district agencies. Soon, the police administration and the fire brigades reached the place of marriage.

Moreover a helicopter from Apollo, Delhi was summoned. I was to take the hurt Chairman to Delhi, who had lost his consciousness. Reena was asked to wait and watch the new developments back home. I got busy with the first aid work.

Montgomery said to me, "Do everything possible to save him. He is not just the Chairman. He is your husband. We all shall obey you. Command us like the mistress of the house."

The ambulance carrying Chairman and me left at a tremendous speed. It was followed by a large caravan of cars on road. All the people who had come to attend the marriage followed the injured by road. They did not know what had happened and what was the mystery?

The elected member said to the headmaster, "We could face a DEO. This Chairman is the virtual chief minister of the state. Let us run away with our families, cross the border and save our skin. Otherwise, she is sure to dig our grave a hundred meter down."

They tried their best to cross the border along with their families. First, they tried to cross to Nepal. For this, they went to Simra, a border town that checked the entry to Kathmandu. But they found police waiting for them everywhere. Then they tried to enter Pakistan through Doda and Kistwar area but the high alert sounded for them forbade them to do so. Finally they made the last unsuccessful effort at Dera Baba Nanak sector where they were nabbed by the armed forces.

'She will know that we did it because we wanted to take revenge.' Thought the culprit duo.

Sudha's mother had taken the poisonous liquid and had been wandering here and there like a person who had lost wits was finally charred to death in the fire with another person.

Since two casualties took place, police sprang into action. The eye witnesses helped the police spot the culprits. The headmaster and the elected member were arrested and finally booked by the police.

Sudha took an overdose of alcohol and was howling like a mad dog at her husband Sunny Sharma. She herself did not know what she was speaking and in the intoxicated stage she confessed her crime how she tried to kill Durga by poisoning the milk to be taken by the bride. It was a self confession of a stark fact and an attempt to murder for which now she was to be tried in the court of law.

The most disgruntled man was Vinod, who had never come across up to his Ph.D thesis such a scene in all fiction, drama, prose or poetry, either in the east or in the west, ancient or modern. He was simply shocked. However, he was a perfect gentleman who understood the turn of destiny and acted accordingly. He felt that since God wanted it, he must obey the same and bow out of the game.

The would be wife of the Chairman was surprised to see her husband to be, in just 5 days, locked up with Durga in an eternal embrace.

She told her friends, "Really, the embrace was the most impassioned one I had ever seen. Vishal did not even touch me in that way despite my many efforts to do something similar. I thought he did not know any of the things of the grown ups, he was a kid. What a turn of events!"

The Apollo people knew where to land the helicopter. I knew when intravenous injections were to be given and after what duration.

All things being intact, the helicopter flew off before some members who were present at the marriage could come to the school premises where the helicopter had landed in the ground and from where it flew off. They could not see the helicopter.

This time Montgomery had also been allowed a seat in the helicopter. Nothing special happened. The pious man was praying most of the time with his eyes closed. I was looking intently at the face of my sweetheart.

Vishal had remembered that he had named me 'Dorris' in America.

At Apollo, as usual a full team of doctors, surgeons and super surgeons were waiting in the operation hall. The last experience had evidently shown prompt payment of this patient.

Otherwise also the patient, his wife and all the people were very co-operative.

Dr. Mongha was smiling when he saw the patient and said to me, taking me for the Chairman's wife, "It is the third patient in my knowledge who is coming back to his normal self. Please observe the old instructions with regard to him.

"The most important is not to deny him anything, not to go cross with him and to love him, care for him and be considerate to him."

He further added, "To my mind, nothing is to be done to him. No operation and not much of medication. Only thing, keep him away from the cares and worries of life. If he responds well, I may discharge him within a week after keeping him under observation for that time. He appears to be okay and my judgment seems never to be wrong. One more thing, he will forget what happened in the intervening period."

Dr. Mongha took a long time with Montgomery and told him the same he had told me.

After a week, the patient was declared fit, and we all left amid jubilations and thrills.

The Chairman had his own bungalow studded with all amenities in the R.K. Puram area, a posh area of Delhi. Montgomery got it done right in case of a medical emergency.

My mother, my brother, Sneha and her husband Harish had been called over to Delhi secretly.

A new bungalow was purchased in R.K. Puram itself in the name of my mother and brother. Montgomery on finding some time alone, told me, "I did whatever I could do for you. The best was that I prayed for you. My prayer coupled with yours has brought results. I want your help. You know I have two marriageable daughters. Before being operated, he had said that he would give some financial support. I did not say anything to him. He was himself sick. Now that the things have been normalised, please help me. I look to you for mercy."

I asked him not to behave like that. I held his hand and said, "Since you are a gentleman and since you have served the organisation and Vishal so dearly, and have made all efforts to save him, please be rest assured I shall personally intervene for your case and get the optimum help. Don't worry, please. Your daughters are my sisters. I shall personally look after their wedding."

I saw the tears of gratitude in the eyes of the pious man!

The hit from bamboo sleeper was more psychological than physical.

The first thing the Chairman asked me after coming completely to himself was, "Have you forgiven me for being outrageous? I beg a hundred thousand apologies." The hospital room number 11 was fresh in his mind.

I only smiled and said, "My darling, it was mutual. You and I committed no sin. The real sin is to break somebody's heart, to swindle and betray somebody. Our hearts had been innocent. God in his mercy will forgive us."

"What is the first thing that I can do to you to atone my sin?" asked the Chairman most solemnly.

"Yes! You can bless me in one way and remove the burden off my soul. Please marry me within the Indian or western traditions with full incantations and all." I said to him imploringly.

The Chairman said, "If only my magic man Montgomery would have been here, I would have fulfilled your wish this very hour."

Just then I called aloud and said, "Montgomery!"

In a moment Montgomery appeared and the Chairman ordered him.

"Montgomery you know, I married her in room number 11 privately because I could not control myself. That was a marriage without marriage. Please find out the best temple or Church and arrange the remarriage in the Indo-Anglican way. All religions are the same and all religions are great. None is higher or lower."

I got dressed in the saree purchased for me at the orders of the Chairman.

The marriage took place with extraordinary fervour and enthusiasm. It was no ordinary marriage. It was the marriage of the biggest business tycoon of northern India and attended by thousands of people. Important among the visitors were Vinod, Reena, and a large numbers of people from Kalka and Solan. The students of the school were most pleased because they got a new Principal, Durga Chadda and also had two holidays in the bargain!

✦ ✦ ✦

Dr. S.K. Sood, retired Principal of Post Graduate Co-Educational College, Pathankot, India, has first-hand experience with frustrated youths and their problems both in the east and the west. For the last four decades, he has been teaching young boys and girls and listening to their love tangles, anguish and exultation, sorrows and thrills. His first novel *Drink Not To Die But Live and Love* is already quite popular in States and other Western Countries.

In this novel, the writer has tried to present the experiences, the travails and tribulations of a young woman through her own point of view in the most original style. Dr. Sood is doctorate in literature and his pen penetrates into the character's hidden recesses easily with great finesse and swiftness.